Praise for *Twice Born*

'This stunning novel about the nature of grief, love and motherhood blew me away with the quality and depth of her haunting story.' *The Bookseller*

'Mazzantini's haunting novel, beautifully written and skillfully crafted, proves that despite the hatred exposed by war, love persists, and even flourishes.' *Publishers Weekly*

'Awash with vivid memories and powerful emotion ... A stunning book.' *Irish News*

'Beautiful but heartbreaking.' *BookPage*

'Epic and captivating ... Truly unforgettable.' *Easy Living*

'*Twice Born* by Margaret Mazzantini is a timeless yet compelling modern tale of love and war ... as gritty, difficult, compelling, and real as the evening news.' DolceDolce

'Mazzantini's depictions of love, maternal and romantic, are powerfully raw.' *Kirkus Reviews*

'Beautifully rendered, *Twice Born* is a testament to love's power over hate and the promise of new beginnings.'

The Daily Beast

'Artfully told ... enraptures its audience with larger-than-life characters travelling along life's twisted journey.'

Meg Talks Books

'Beautiful, lyrical, painful ... It also illuminates, for at its heart is the power of love, which does not conquer all, but is the only means for the soul to survive and heal. Highly recommended.'

The Best Damn Creative Writing Blog

'A stunning story of love and war, of violence and of the secrets within a family.'   Le Monde des Livres

'Margaret Mazzantini expertly weaves together jealousy, horror, money, cynicism, compassion, madness, and hope.'   *Le Journal du Dimanche*

'Splendid and engaging ... page after page of images, rhythm, suspense, suffering, and synchrony. Pure energy.'

La Nazione

ABOUT THE AUTHOR

Margaret Mazzantini was born in Dublin and lives in Rome
with her husband and four children. She made her literary
début in 1994 with *Il catino di zinco* (*The Zinc Basin*), followed
by *Manola* (1999), and in 2001 she published *Non ti muovere*
(*Don't Move*), which won multiple awards, including the
Premio Strega, Premio Grinzane Cavour, Premio Città di
Bari, and European Zepter Prize, and in 2004 was made into
an acclaimed film directed by Sergio Castellitto and starring
Penélope Cruz. After the theatrical monologue *Zorro* (2002),
Mazzantini published the novel *Venuto al mondo* (*Twice Born*,
2008, published by Oneworld Publications in 2011), which
won the prestigious Premio Campiello in 2009, and was
made into a film directed by Sergio Castellitto, starring
Penélope Cruz and Emile Hirsch (2012). This was followed
by *Nessuno si salva da solo* (*No One Survives Alone*, 2011) and
Mare al mattino (*Morning Sea*, 2011), the latter winning the
Premio Cesare Pavese and Premio Matteotti awards. Her
most recent novel is *Splendore* (*Splendour*, 2013). Margaret
Mazzantini's books are international bestsellers, and have
been translated into more than thirty languages.

ALSO AVAILABLE IN ENGLISH
FROM MARGARET MAZZANTINI

Don't Move
Twice Born

Morning Sea

MARGARET MAZZANTINI

Translated by Ann Gagliardi

ONEWORLD

A Oneworld book

First published in North America, Great Britain, and Australia by
Oneworld Publications, 2015
Originally published in Italian as *Mare al mattino* by Einaudi, 2011

ISBN 978-1-78074-633-3
eBook ISBN 978-1-78074-634-0

This book has been selected to receive financial assistance from English PEN's
"PEN Translates!" programme, supported by Arts Council England. English
PEN exists to promote literature and our understanding of it, to uphold writers'
freedoms around the world, to campaign against the persecution and
imprisonment of writers for stating their views, and to promote the friendly
co-operation of writers and the free exchange of ideas. www.englishpen.org

Typeset in Bembo by Hewer Text UK Ltd, Edinburgh
Printed and bound in Great Britain by
CPI Group (UK) Ltd, Croydon, CR0 4YY

Oneworld Publications
10 Bloomsbury Street
London WC1B 3SR
England

For you with Dhaki on the *coche pequeño*

CONTENTS

Farid and the Gazelle

Farid has never seen the sea, never gone in.

He's imagined it many times. Dotted with stars like a pasha's cloak, blue like the blue wall of the dead city.

He's looked for fossilized seashells buried millions of years ago when the sea extended into the desert. He's chased after fish lizards that swim beneath the sand. He's seen the salty lake and the bitter lake and silvery camels advancing like shabby pirate ships. He lives in an oasis on the edge of the Sahara.

His ancestors belonged to a tribe of Bedouin nomads. They set up their tents in wadis, riverbeds covered with vegetation. The goats grazed; the wives cooked on fiery stones. They never left the desert. They didn't entirely trust the coastal people, merchants, and pirates. The desert was their home – their open, limitless sea of sand, mottled by the dunes like a jaguar's coat. They possessed nothing, only footprints, which the sand covered over. The sun moved the shadows. They were accustomed to withstanding thirst, drying out like dates without dying. A camel opened the way for them with its long, crooked shadow. They disappeared in the dunes.

We are invisible to the world, but not to God.

They moved from place to place with this thought in their hearts.

In winter, the northern wind that crossed the ocean of rocks stiffened the woollen shawls on their bodies. Their skin, bloodless like the goatskins stretched taut across their drums, clung to their bones. Ancient curses fell from the sky. The fault lines in the sand were blades. Touching the desert brought wounds.

Their elders were buried where they died, left to the silence of the sand. Afterwards, the Bedouins set out again, fringes of white and indigo cloth.

In spring, new dunes emerged, rosy and pale. Sand virgins.

The searing ghibli wind drew near, accompanied by the jackal's hoarse cry. Here and there, little tendrils of wind nipped at the sand like wandering spirits. Rough squalls followed, as sharp as scimitars. An army brought back to life. In a flash, the desert rose to devour the sky and there was no longer any border with the hereafter. The Bedouins bent beneath the weight of the grey tempest, protecting themselves against the bodies of animals that had fallen to their knees as if beneath the shroud of some ancient judgement.

Then they stopped, built a wall of clay, an enclosed pasture. Wheels left furrows in the sand.

Now and then, a caravan passed through. The settlement lay on the route used by merchants who cut across the desert from black Africa to the sea. They carried ivory, resin, precious stones and captives to sell as slaves in the ports of Cyrenaica and Tripolitania.

The merchants rested in the oasis, ate, drank. A city was born, with roofs of palm and walls of dried clay reminiscent of braided rope. The women lived above the men, separate. They walked barefoot across the roofs and went to the well with terracotta jars on their heads. They mixed couscous with lamb innards. They prayed on the tombs of marabouts, of holy men. At sunset, they danced on the roofs to the sound of the nay, their bellies moving like drowsy snakes. On the ground, the men made bricks, bartered, played tawla and smoked the narghile.

That city is no longer there. Nothing remains but a sketch, a sanctuary eaten by the wind of sand. Next to it, a new city arose, built for Colonel Gaddafi by foreign architects from the East. Cement buildings, aerials.

Along the roads, there are huge images of the colonel, here pictured in desert camouflage, there as a devout Muslim or a military official. In some, he's imperious and grave; in others, he smiles with open arms.

People sit on empty petrol cans, bony children, old men sucking roots to freshen their mouths. Electrical wires travel limply from one building to the next. The searing ghibli bears plastic bags and litter left behind by desert tourists.

There's no work, just sugary drinks and goats and dates to can for export.

Many of the young leave to find work in the oil reserves, the black blocks on the map, the eternal flames of the desert.

It's not a real city. It's an aggregation of lives.

Farid lives in the old city, in one of those low houses with doors all round the same central court, a wild garden, a gate that's always open. He walks to school, runs on his thin legs with their skin that peels like the bark on reeds. His mother, Jamila, wraps sesame sticks in paper for his snack.

After school, he and his friends play with a little old cart that drags tin cans, or else football. He rolls like a grub in the red dust. He steals little bananas and bunches of black dates. With the help of a rope, he climbs high into the heart of those trees full of shadows.

Round his neck, he wears an amulet, a little leather pouch stuffed with beads and a few tufts of animal fur. All children wear them.

Evil eyes will look at the amulet. You will be safe, his mother explained.

Omar, Farid's father, is a technician. He installs TV aerials. He waits for the signal, smiling at the women who don't want to miss the next episode of the Egyptian soap opera and treat him like a saviour of dreams. Jamila is jealous of those stupid women. She studied singing, but her husband won't let her perform during weddings or at festivals, let alone for tourists. So Jamila sings for Farid, her only spectator in the rooms full of drapes and rugs and smelling of sagebrush and herbs beneath the domed plaster roof of their house.

Farid is in love with his mother and her arms, which make a breeze like palm leaves, and the smell of her breath when she sings one of her maloufs full of love and tears, and her heart swells so much that she has to hold it tight so it won't fall into the rusty iron rainwater basin that's always dry.

His mother is young, like a sister. Sometimes they play bride and groom. Farid combs her hair, adjusts her veil.

Jamila's forehead is a round stone; her eyes are rimmed like a bird's; her lips are two sweet, ripe dates.

It's a sunset with no wind. The sky is peach-coloured.

Farid leans against the wall in his garden. He studies his feet, the filthy toes sticking out of his sandals.

A flurry of new moss is growing in one of the cracks in the wall. Farid bends to smell the fresh scent. Only then does he realize that an animal is breathing beside him, so close that he can't move. His heart leaps into his eyes.

He's afraid it might be a uaddan, a legendary creature, part sheep, part donkey, with big horns. His grandfather told him it sometimes appears on the horizon between two dunes, an evil mirage. It's been a long time since anyone has seen a uaddan, but Grandfather Mussa swears the creature still hides in the black sandstone wadi, where living things are unable to survive. Grandfather Mussa says the uaddan's very angry about all the jeeps ruining the desert, damaging it with their wheels.

But the animal doesn't have white tufts and lunar horns, and she's not grinding her teeth. She has a sand-coloured coat and horns so thin they look like twigs. The animal gazes at Farid. She may be hungry.

Farid realizes it's a gazelle, a young gazelle. She doesn't run away. Her eyes, wide and so near, are lustrous and calm. Her coat shivers with a sudden tremor. Maybe the animal is trembling, just like Farid. But the gazelle is also too curious to move away. Farid slowly moves a branch towards her. The gazelle opens a mouth full of flat white teeth and tears off a few fresh pistachios, then backs away in her tracks without taking her eyes off Farid. All of a sudden, she turns, jumps over the earthen wall, and runs over the horizon of the dunes, kicking up sand.

At school the next day, Farid fills pages with gazelles. He draws them crookedly in pencil, then jabs his finger in tempera paint to colour them in.

★   ★   ★

The television is broadcasting a continuous loop of the film the colonel produced with Anthony Quinn starring as the legendary Omar Mukhtar, the Bedouin leader who fought like a lion against the Italian invaders. Farid is proud. He can feel his heart beating in his bones. His father's name is Omar, like the desert hero.

Farid and his friends play war with blowguns made from reeds that spit out pistachios and red rocks left behind by storms.

You're dead! You're dead!

They fight on, because no one wants to throw himself to the ground and end the game.

Farid knows that war has broken out somewhere.

His parents whisper until late at night, and his friends say weapons have arrived from the frontier. They saw them being unloaded from jeeps at night. They'd like to have an AK-47 or a rocket launcher, too.

They fire off a few Bengal flares beside the old deaf beggar.

Farid jumps around and has so much fun.

Hisham, his youngest uncle, a university student in Benghazi, has joined the rebel forces.

Grandfather Mussa, who works as a guide taking tourists to the Cursed Mountain, and knows how to recognize snake tracks and read rock drawings, says Hisham is stupid, that he's read too many books.

He says the colonel has paved Libya over with tarmac and cement, filled it with black Tuaregs from Mali, carved the words of that ridiculous green book of his on every wall, met with bankers and politicians the world over, his escort of beautiful women in tow as if he were an actor on holiday. But he's a Bedouin just like them, a man of the desert. He defended their race, which was persecuted by history, pushed back to the edges of the oases. Better him than the Muslim Brotherhood.

Hisham said, *Freedom is better.*

Omar climbs onto the roof to adjust the satellite dish. They manage to get a channel that isn't scrambled by the regime. The coastal cities are burning. Now they know that the prophet of a united Africa is firing upon his Jamahiriya, his peopledom. At this point, he's alone in the halls of power. When Grandfather Mussa sees Misurata destroyed, he tears his print of the colonel off the wall and throws it under the bed.

The telegram comes. Hisham has lost his sight – a shrapnel wound to the face. He won't use his eyes to read books any more. Everyone cries; everyone prays. Hisham is in the hospital in Benghazi. At least he's alive. He's not in a green bag like Fatima's son.

On the streets, people scratch the colonel's words

from the walls, cover them with slogans of liberty and caricatures of the Big Rat and his fake medals. Rocks decapitate the statue at the entrance to the medina.

It's nighttime. There's nothing but a little bare light that won't stop trembling as if from a cough. Omar empties a bag onto the table. There's money inside, all the dinars from Omar's savings, plus the euros and dollars Grandfather Mussa has earned with the tourists in the desert. Omar counts the money, then pulls out a stone and hides it in the wall. He talks with Jamila, clutches her little hands in his own. Farid isn't sleeping. He looks at that knot of hands wavering in the dark like a coconut in the rain.

Omar says they have to go. That they should have gone a while ago. There's no future in the desert. Now there's war. He's afraid for the child.

Farid thinks his father is wrong to be afraid for him. He's ready for war, just like Uncle Hishram. He's covered his eyes with his hands to see what it's like to be blind. You bang into things, but it doesn't matter.

Farid leans against the wall in his garden.

The gazelle always comes noiselessly – a light leap and there she is, with her rimmed eyes, her diamond-shaped pupils, her ears with their light, tufty fur, and her bone horns, little and coiled. They've become friends. Farid hasn't told anyone about her. But he's always worried someone will find out, terrified someone will catch her. She's young and overly trusting, taking risks, coming too far into the residential area. She ventures along, tension beneath her coat, quivering muscles primed to bound away, not to stay. Each time they have to get accustomed to trusting. They belong to the same desert but to different races. Farid presses himself back against the wall and waits for the gazelle to breathe out of her dark nostrils so that he can breathe with her. She moves her muzzle. She wants to play. Once, when she sits on her hind legs, it looks like his mother at sunset, the same regal pose.

It's a spring morning. Omar is working on the roof. He connects electrical cables and waits for a spark, the signal that the soap opera is safe. These days, the electricity comes and goes in hiccups. The women don't want to think about the war; they want to cry over love. They want to find out whether the good man will learn that his son is really his and whether the bad man will plummet over the cliff in his black car.

Farid saw Omar step backwards on the roof, vainly

seek for something to grab on to, stumble, stand back up. Other men have climbed up on the village roofs, men in camouflage outfits and yellow hats. They look like construction workers, but they shoot, aiming low at the people in the market, who run and yell. The men are loyalist troops. Many are foreigners, *murtaziqa*, paid mercenaries from other, sub-Saharan wars. When they shoot, they yell like in the movies. A half-naked soldier crouches to do his business. Maybe he drank too much tamarind juice, or maybe he's scared. Now he fires like that, trousers down.

Omar stayed to watch them. He tried to speak, to stop them. They put a rifle down his throat. *Fight with us or you're dead.* Farid saw his father slide towards the rain gutter. He was missing a shoe. Farid could see one of the beige socks Jamila mended in the evenings. The men put a pistol into his father's hands. Omar shot into the sky towards the birds that weren't there. Then he let the pistol fall. The man without trousers pushed Farid's father off the roof.

Farid saw the pick-up trucks with machine guns and bazookas and dirty, wild faces, green flags wrapped round their heads. They even killed the animals to scare the people.

Fortunately, the gazelle wasn't there that day. She only came when it was quiet.

Jamila waited for night to fall, night that is never as dark as one thinks. The full moon lit up the sandhills and the palm groves, the buildings, and the clay houses with their spiky points against the evil eye.

She hid Farid in the root cellar with the tealeaves and hanging dried meat. All around came lightning bursts of fire, shots, the smell of burning petrol in the sand.

She dragged her husband's body into the courtyard and washed it with water from the well.

Omar's hair is thick. When it's wet, it looks like bunches of grapes. Jamila cleans his ears, clutches his hair. *It's a blessing, my love. This way, it will be easier for the angels to take you, to carry you into the sky.* There's an old desert belief that the innocent dead are dragged up to heaven by their hair.

In the gardens around theirs, other women are praying and crying. Some families were taken hostage, used as human shields.

When morning comes, Omar's body is no longer there.

Jamila whispers through the clay walls. She talks with their ancestors, asks their advice for the journey.

★   ★   ★

Farid comes out of the root cellar. He smells that strange smell, the unguent for the dead. He looks at the freshly turned dirt in the garden, the broken swing his father didn't fix in time.

He gathers his things, a notebook, his red sweater for winter.

He looks at the picture of his grandfather sitting on a camel in front of the oasis, his grandfather in his white turban and glasses, sandals on his thin feet. Grandfather writes the Qur'an on wooden panels. He knows the ancient fables and the big battles with the Romans and the Turks. He told Farid about the Red Castle and the pirates. He walks with a limp because he stepped on a mine left behind after the war against Chad. Sometimes he brings Farid to the desert with him. Farid has seen the worm-eaters, the rock drawings of elephants and antelopes and of simple handprints. Once, they got lost. Grandfather Mussa told him that real Bedouins die in the desert, enfolded in a swirling sandstorm. He said that it was the best thing one could hope for, that God caused them to get lost in order to reunite them with their destiny. *The desert is like a beautiful woman. It never reveals itself but appears and disappears. Its face changes shape and colour, volcanic black or white as salt. An invisible horizon that dances and moves like its dunes.*

★   ★   ★

Farid saw Jamila move the rock and take the money, which she wrapped close to her body with a piece of cloth. He heard the sound of her chattering teeth.

She packed some things in an Adidas bag.

Farid looked for the gazelle through the wooden slats. He wanted to say goodbye, smell her breath in the mud enclosure in the garden.

They left at dawn. Jamila kissed the stone slab in front of the door. Farid thought of the smell of certain afternoons when his mother took off her veil and danced barefoot, in her bra. Her little belly, shining with argan oil, moved like earth, like earth vibrating with life, the centre of the house, the stone of salvation.

Jamila snatches the key from the door and tucks it away. They run between houses and clouds of smoke, sliding along like rats. The war is the next block over. Bullet streaks burn the sky. The key falls in the dirt. His mother doesn't bend to pick it up.

'It doesn't matter, Farid. We have to hurry.'

'And how will Father get back in?'

'He'll call a blacksmith.'

Jamila has not told him that Omar is an angel buried within the desert.

★　　★　　★

Farid looks around. What's happened to his friends, to the bumper cars beneath the canopy, to the ice kiosk, and the sunglasses stand?

At the city gate, it's like a fair. They see people with eyes like animals'. Sweat pours from their heads, from their noses. Everyone is yelling and looking for something. Beyond the gate lies the desert. Jamila and Farid queue with the others, people with rolled-up mattresses on their backs and suitcases that won't fit on the buses.

Many hope to find safety in the refugee camps across the border. Jamila knows that's a dangerous journey. The loyalist forces control kilometres of barbed wire and fire on the fugitives.

They will go towards the sea. The truck is full of packages and black men packed in like slaves. It almost neglects to stop to pick them up. Jamila yells and follows it. The two of them clamber aboard as quickly as they can. Farid scrambles up first, like a monkey, then her.

Farid sees a jeep with flaming wheels barrel over an old man. It's the first thing he sees in the desert.

He can't keep his eyes open. His mother puts her veil over his face to keep out the sand. The wheels of the truck go up and down the dunes.

Kilometres of silence, nothing but the growl of the motor. It's a war scene from any war. Human beings deported like beasts. They don't stop to piss.

They all have their eyes closed, heads low and white with sand.

The horizon is viscous. The ghibli shakes its soot-dirtied surface. They see carcasses of burnt cars, litter blowing in the wind.

Grandfather Mussa told him that everything that ends up in the desert belongs to the desert, that it means something because it can be used for another purpose, another life.

Colourful rags appear on the sand like clothes spread to dry on the ground – a shirt, a pair of empty-looking blue jeans. A bit further on, there's a shoe.

Then they see heads sunken into the sand and devoured by the heat. Hair. Jawbones. Hands like dried carob beans.

On the truck, everyone yells, and then everyone is silent. Jamila leans over the side to throw up. Farid has the veil over his eyes. He sees the open-air cemetery through that pale filter.

They are all black Africans. Dead for months already, from before the war. Their clothes are intact, no bullet holes.

Everyone on the truck knows they were migrants from Mali, Ghana, Niger, abandoned in the desert after the colonel struck a deal with the Europeans to block the flow of desperate illegal immigrants.

God in the desert is water and shade.

An empty bottle lies beside one fleshless hand. The last gesture before death.

Where is God in this desert?

Jamila is thirsty. Thirst. She rummages in her bag, dumps water on her son's head, pulls the veil away from his mouth. She quenches his thirst, pulls him to her. *Drink, Farid. Drink.*

They are the only two left in the world.

The house is an abandoned clay egg behind them.

Then, bushes, some of them with white buds. A salt bush. The air is milder. The ghibli roars listlessly, a tired feline in retreat.

It's the pre-desert zone. Rows of grapevines. Dry and crumbling stone walls. Abandoned cottages like something out of the Tuscan countryside. It's one of the old rural villages where the Italian colonists lived. A grove of crooked olive trees. Archways opening onto nothing.

There's sand in the engine. The truck stops. The driver has a covered Tuareg face, his red ancient eyes yell at them to get off the truck. All of a sudden comes the roar of an explosion so near it interrupts his yell. And yet the sky is calm. A flock of messenger birds passes in a mobile drawing. The Tuareg is talking on his mobile phone, shouting in Tamashek. Farid doesn't understand.

The sun climbs higher into the sky. They've been waiting for two hours. Farid and Jamila walk through the ghost town looking for relief. There's a square, an old town hall. They go into the church. The roof has collapsed. The apse is disfigured. The floor is earthen with a few bricks. They rest against a wall, share the bread. Jamila prays. It's not a mosque, but it doesn't matter. It's shade where people have knelt to speak with the voice of silence.

One of the black men has taken off his shoes. His foot is swollen like a skinned ram. He's from the savannah. He's walked for days. He's afraid of gangrene. He complains. A Somali man helps him. He holds his knife in the flame of his lighter. He cuts the man's foot, then wraps it in a leaf, like dates before they're closed into a box for tourists.

They start walking again.

The rumble of a motor. A quad bike appears on the horizon.

A fat man is driving it. He's wearing a T-shirt with a Pepsi bottle on it and words underneath, *Ishrab Pepsi*.

Farid looks at the T-shirt that triggers a thirst from another world.

The man takes over the package tour group. He will lead them to the sea.

They all walk behind the quad bike, which looks like some kind of lunar tractor. The black man drags his foot wrapped in green. One person drops a mattress; another drops a cooking pan. Too heavy. They proceed in absolute silence. Before, they talked, but now, no. There's no sound but the moans of a pregnant woman, though she seems stronger than the men. She conceals her condition beneath black layers of cloth, fearful perhaps that she'll be left behind.

A line of cockroaches crosses the dunes.

They leave the ancient track of wandering Bedouins, a trail of footprints the sand will sweep away. They've returned to their destiny – finding their way in nothingness.

Grandfather Mussa didn't want to leave. He stayed in the garden, his feet soaking in a basin, and watched the eagles on the lookout for lizards in the desert.

Jamila is not sad. She sinks, catches her breath before a new wall of sand. Farid is on her shoulders now, wrapped in a womb of cloth, like when he was little.

Jamila is young, just past twenty. A young widow with her child. The desert is their seashell.

Farid wears an amulet round his neck.

The horizon changes. It is punctuated by sun-baked greenery, a wall of carob trees. Oleanders in bloom line their gradual descent.

Farid has never smelled this smell before, wild and deep.

Is this how the sea smells, the bright expanses and blue depths?

Now they all run, heads low between thorny prickly pears. Farid jumps off Jamila's shoulders, leaves his little camel. He runs and rolls between the sand and the tamarisks. It's the first time he's left the desert.

A hand gathering money on the beach, another man in a turban but wearing city clothes, his pale jacket damp with sweat at the neck and on his shoulders. The fat man yells. The bottle of Pepsi jiggles on his soft belly. They have to hurry. They're out in the open. Though of course the situation is under control. The colonel's henchmen have given orders to allow the boats to leave. Now the colonel wants desperate people to fill the

Mediterranean and strike fear into European hearts. This is his best weapon, the rotten flesh of the poor. It's dynamite. It blows up the refugee centres and the hypocrisy of governments.

Now on the beach, they're all protesting.

They look in dismay at the rusty hulk on the water. It looks like an overturned bus, not a motorboat.

They yell and shake their heads.

The boat is too expensive, too old. The boat is a wreck.

The man in city clothes says, *What did you expect, a cruise ship?* He shouts that the deal is off. He'll find another bunch of boatpeople to cram onto this boat, people who aren't as stupid as they are. He shakes his arm, says they have to leave, clear out, go back into the bushes, the desert. He spits on the ground and says he hasn't got time to waste on rats.

He throws the money onto the sand. A young man picks it up, but the city man wants nothing more to do with it. He climbs onto the jeep. The young man follows him, begs through the window, *Please, for Allah.* There are many women in the group, including his pregnant wife. He asks the city man if he has children. The city man opens the door of the jeep straight into him. He steps forward and puts the money in his wallet. This time no one breathes a word. The human trafficker walks across the sand in his shiny shoes. He opens the trunk of the jeep and flings plastic-wrapped packs of bottled water onto the sand. *I thought you might be thirsty.* Everyone thanks him. Jamila grabs a boiling-hot bottle of water and slips it into her bag.

Farid looks at the sea for the first time in his life. He touches it with his feet, gathers it up in his hands. He drinks it and spits it out.

He thinks it's big, but not big like the desert. It ends where the sky begins, just beyond that horizontal blue line.

He had thought you could walk on it like pirate ships. Instead, it's wet and sucks you under. The waves move back and forth like the clothes on his mother's clothesline; if he runs away, they come after him.

The pregnant woman lifts her dress to step into the water but ends up wet to the neck. She opens a thin mouthful of too-big teeth. She looks like a camel that's scared of a fire.

Everyone climbs, pushes, scrambles aboard.

The boat sinks lower and lower.

Two boys from Malawi, quicker on the uptake than the others, walk with bare feet like sailors. They check out the inside of the boat, open the tanks held tight with bungee cords in the stern, stick in their noses to make sure the tanks really hold diesel fuel. The fat man yells that they are damned sons of bitches, *ifriqiyyun*, slaves who've escaped from the oasis ghettos. He programmes their route on the GPS and leaps off the boat, getting wet up to his belt. His hand thumps the side of the boat. *Good luck, sons of bitches*.

Farid looks at the sea, clear and smooth like a pale blue earthenware tile. He looks for fish, their backs. The first bits of their new life. Jamila kisses him and fiddles with his hair. *How long will the trip last?*

Not long. Just enough time for a lullaby.

Jamila starts singing with her nightingale voice, whistling and imitating the sound of the zukra. Her voice lowers to the sea. Then she falls asleep. Her slender head like a gazelle's, like a big sister's. Farid finds a space amid all the bodies and looks back. The coast isn't there any more, nothing but the sea, rising and falling. He remembers his house, the swing, the majolica tiles round the well with their rust- and emerald-coloured drawings. He thinks of the gazelle. She came and went as she wished. Always at sunset. She had started to eat from his hand. He'd pluck dates and pistachios and serve them to the animal, his open palm a plate. He thinks of the sound and then of the smell of the gazelle's mouth.

There were spots on the inside, on her tongue. She smelled of wadi, of a recent flow of water through the dust. The best muzzle on earth, apart from his mother's. That last day, he'd hugged her. He hadn't even known he wouldn't see her again, her burnt beige coat that lit up at sunset. Her fur smelled like a rug, the same smell Farid smelled in the desert when he pitched the tent with Grandfather Mussa and they slept on the prayer mat.

He doesn't mind leaving the past. He's a child. He's too young to have any real sense of time. What he knows and what awaits him are all in the same hand.

First, he's excited; then he's scared; then he's tired; then nothing more. He threw up. Now there's nothing left. The sun follows them like a ravenous tongue, dripping on their heads, suffocating heat, sweat.

The sea is monotonous. There's never anything new. Looking at it is a mistake; it's like looking at a headless animal with an infinity of shaking humps, blue flesh spraying foam from its submerged mouth. Farid looks for that head that never surfaces, just comes close and then disappears.

He wonders about the face of the sea. What does it look like?

One of the Somali men fired at the waves a while ago to test a flare. It didn't work. The flares are rotten, like the boat. The young man drank too much with his friends. They burnt their stomachs and their brains. Now they're punching each other.

Everyone is pale, grey as a rag. All of them have thrown up. The vomit flows along the worn wood floor with the heaving of the sea.

Jamila tells her son that he has to keep his eyes on a point on the horizon to keep from feeling seasick.

Farid rummages in the bottom of the bit of sky where the sun melts the horizon.

Black diesel smoke from the engine blows into his face. His mother holds him tight. He seeks that contact, her smell. But Jamila is permeated with diesel, the smell of this journey, the smell of their hope.

Farid's eyes hurt. His legs hurt. The sea is crosswise now, the boat leaning entirely to one side. They can't move from the spaces they have been assigned, each in their own holes among the bodies. A little girl whimpers. Two men yell in a dialect Farid doesn't know. The heat is suffocating. The sun burns sores on their lips. His mother rations the water. She gives him smaller and smaller sips, not even enough to clean his tongue. They do their business in a common bucket that gets emptied into the sea. Animals? It's beyond that. Animals aren't as afraid of death as they are. The sea is a world unto itself, a world within the world, with its own laws, its own strength. It expands. It rises. The boat is like the shell of a dead scarab beetle, the kind Farid used to find in the desert, killed by the ghibli. Farid feels the sun inside his head. It won't go away, not even when he closes his eyes. He thinks of the wild caper leaves his mother would chew and put on his forehead when he was ill. He thinks of the man who sells prickly pears, his quick, magic gesture when he peeled them.

Jamila crumbles a sesame stick into Farid's mouth, but his throat is a wall of sand.

The sea is a mountain that rises. Farid is scared of those watery dunes. The engine toils like a dying camel.

At night, it's cold. The temperature goes down with the water. The water becomes black paper. It lets off mist that lingers and makes them damp. Farid is shivering. He's wrapped now in his mother's veil, and he's cold beneath the slippery, damp cloth. The hateful wind whips at him. Farid clings to his mother's bones, trying to find the heat of her bosom. She is shivering, too, like a basket of nervous snakes. It's been a long while since she let him near her breasts. *You're a big boy.* Now she pushes him there, where some of the day's warmth has remained, like on the rocks in the desert. In the end, it's a blessing they have to huddle so close together, a blessing like the wind and sea. Farid sleeps. He thinks about the big palm leaves where he always took shelter when it started to rain. One day, Aghib, the old man who sits in the sun sewing Berber shoes for tourists, told him that everything that had happened in their country was the fault of oil, that if it weren't for the black sea beneath the desert, no dictator would want to dictate laws and no foreigners would come to defend them with their cruise missiles. Old Aghib pointed at him, his calloused finger riddled with needle holes. *Oil is the devil's shit. Don't trust things that seem like blessings. It's worse than a monkey trap. Whenever something is a blessing for the rich, it's bad luck for the poor.*

That didn't stop Farid from trusting the gazelle that brought her muzzle all the way to his doorstep to eat from his hands.

It's dark, and the moon is gone. The man filling the engine with diesel uses his lighter to see. He staggers, then swears as the damp sea air douses the flame. Farid's mother's arms are not so strong now. They give way, like the boat, like wheels in the desert.

Farid waits for sunrise. He waits for Italy, where women go around with their heads uncovered and there's an infinity of channels on television. They will step off the boat into the lights. Someone will take pictures, give them toys, Coca-Cola, pizza.

Rashid, Grandfather Mussa's father, had already made this journey at the beginning of the last century, when the Italians burnt villages and chased the Bedouins from the oases and closed them in pens, packed in like goats. Rashid was light-hearted. He played the tabla and gathered resin from rubber trees. His brothers died during the deportation, and he was put onto a ship and sent into exile on a chain of islands with the name Tremiti. No one heard from him again. No one ever knew anything about his death or his new life.

Farid looks at the sea.

Grandfather Mussa told Farid about his father's voyage.

A sandstorm rose; a wind of grey powder swept the coast, as if the desert were rebelling against that cruel exodus. The Bedouins boarding the boats wore dirty tunics, their faces hollowed by months of starvation, the sorrow-filled and vacant eyes of a herd pushed into nothingness.

Once, Mussa, as an adult, travelled all the way to the port his father left from, in a Toyota that belonged to some desert archaeologists, a group of kids from Bologna. They slept together in the old Tuareg camps, visited the Garamante necropolis and the white labyrinths of Ghadames.

From the Gulf of Sirte, Mussa looked at the sea that had swallowed up his father. He thought about setting sail, going to find Rashid in Italy and presenting himself, tall and elegant, with his English bone glasses and his white djellaba. He dreamt of picking up his old father in his arms and bringing him back to his desert on a camel.

The rust of homesickness scratched Mussa's teeth like sand.

But all that blue scared him. It was as if a hand were pulling him backwards by the neck. The ancient terror of the sea.

But he did have time to see a group of half-naked tourists on the beach. They were drinking lime juice and eating blackberries from a basket made of woven leaves.

He came back with his story, which became more risqué over time, the women more naked and inviting, like virgins of paradise.

Farid looks at the sea and thinks of paradise.

His grandfather told him that the women there are more beautiful, the food tastier, and all the colours brighter, because Allah is the painter of the dawn.

Farid thinks of the picture hanging in the dining room of his father, Omar. The photographer retouched it with markers, made the lips redder, the gaze more intense.

Farid's father doesn't look anything like the legendary Omar Mukhtar. He doesn't have any political ideas. He's shy and has weak nerves.

Farid looks at the sea.

Tears leave his eyes and slowly meander through the tiny, salt-whitened hairs on his face.

The Colour of Silence

Vito scrambles over sea cliffs, descends into sandy coves. He's left the village behind him, the noise of a radio, a woman hollering in dialect. Now it's just wind and waves leaping high against the rocks, extending their paws like angry beasts, foaming, retreating. Vito likes the stormy sea. When he was a little boy, he'd jump in and let it slap him around. His mother, Angelina, back on the beach, would yell herself hoarse. She looked tiny as she stood there waving her arms like a marionette. She was such a little thing, with her dress flapping around her legs. The sea was stronger. Take a running start, ride the fast wave, slide as if on soap, be swallowed up by it, bang against the angry throat of the vortex. He'd roll, sand and big rocks tumbling him about on the murky bottom and leaving him dizzy. Sea in his nose, his belly, waves sucking him backwards, scaring him.

Real joy always contains some fear.

These were his best memories – his bathing suit full of sand, his eyes wounded and red, his hair like seaweed. Becoming a weightless rag, trembling with happiness and fear, lips blue, fingers numb. He'd come out for a little while, running, and throw himself down upon the warm sand, trembling and shivering like a mullet in its death throes. Then he'd dive back in, his brain devoid of thought, feeling more fish than human. So what if he didn't make it back? That would be that. What was waiting for him back onshore, anyway? His angry mother, smoking. His grandmother's octopus stew. His summer homework, nasty stuff, because there's nothing worse than books and notebooks in the summer. And he always gets bad grades, an eternal debt of credits to make up.

One time when Angelina was trying to get him out of the water, she stepped on a sea urchin and lost her sunglasses. That time, she slapped him silly. Pulled him out of the water by his hair, banged him around like an octopus. That was the time he'd most hated her, the time he'd felt she loved him more than anything. That night, she let him sleep in her bed, in the crumpled white sheets, with her, her smell, her movements. His mother had separated from his father. At night, she'd stand in front of the door, beneath the palm tree, and smoke, an arm across her belly, the cigarette packet clutched in her hand. She'd talk to herself, moving her lips in silence. Her hair plastered to her forehead, making funny faces. She looked like a monkey ready to leap.

Now Vito is grown. They live outside Catania and come to the island only in the summer and sometimes at Easter. These are the last days of the holidays. His mother has to get back for the start of the school year. Vito has finished school. He's done with the hassle of lies and copying off other kids, waking up at seven in the morning with bad breath. He passed the school-leaving exam. It took tutors, it took prodding, but he passed. He did a good job. *The examiners liked him.* He presented a history paper on the Tripolini, the Italians that Gaddafi banished from Tripoli in 1970. Vito's research started with General Graziani, the butcher who led Mussolini's troops in Libya, and ended with his own mother.

He talked about *mal d'afrique*, the nostalgia that turns sticky, like tar, and about the trip they took together, back in time. To Libya.

It was a total liberation. The next day, he took the biggest dump ever. He went out to celebrate in a club and kissed a girl. Too bad that afterwards she told him she'd made a mistake. Vito managed all the same to explore her mouth, and swelled up and trembled like when he was a kid in the waves.

Now Vito looks at the sea. He's barefoot. He has prehensile feet, calloused like a sailor's. It always happens at the end of the summer. His feet are ready to stay, to live bare on the cliffs and rocks.

It's been a mindless summer, truly vacant. He slept late, swam infrequently. He'd go down to the sea in a daze. He read a few books in the cave as crabs climbed and retreated.

Today, he's wearing a T-shirt and trousers. It's windy.

Vito looks at the debris, pieces of boats and other remnants vomited up onto the beach that looks like a maritime rubbish dump.

There's a war across the sea.

It's been a tragic summer for the island. The same old tragedy, more this year.

Vito hasn't gone into town very often. He's seen the immigrant detention centre. It's bursting at the seams and stinks like a zoo. He's seen queues of the poor souls lined up outside the camp kitchen and the plastic toilet booths. He's seen the fields at night, sown with silver blankets. He saw Tindara, their neighbour, scream and almost die of fright when a Tunisian slipped into her house to steal. He saw kids he knew when he was little, kids he doesn't say hello to any more, making cauldrons of couscous for the Arab lunch of the wretches.

Vito doesn't know what he wants to do with his life. He'd like to study art, something he thought of this summer and hasn't told anyone yet. He draws well. It's the only thing he's always managed to do easily, naturally. Maybe because reason doesn't come into it – all he has to do is follow his hand. Maybe because he spent so much time doodling in notebooks and on school desks instead of studying.

He looks at the remains of a boat, a flank with blue and green stripes, a star, and an Arab moon.

He hasn't eaten a single slice of tuna this summer, not one sea bream. Just eggs and spaghetti. He doesn't like to think about what the fish eat. He dreamt about it one night, the dark depths and a school of fish inside a human skull as if it were a cave full of fluttering sea anemones.

Until last summer he always went fishing. He'd tie a sack of mussels and scraps to a buoy. At sunrise, he'd find octopuses who had glued themselves to the bag and were trying to get inside it with their tentacles. If the octopuses were big, it would be a struggle. They'd suck onto him and he'd have to tear them off. At night, he'd go after squids with a fishing light. He'd use his fishing rod in the port, a spear in the caves. He loved wresting flesh from the sea.

This summer, there's nothing that could make him go snorkelling. He's spent his time on the hammock and only gone into town if he really had to. Too much sorrow. Too much chaos. But there's still one part of the island that's remained untouched by the world, just a few steps away from where the boats land and from the news crews.

Vito looks at the sea. One day, his mother said, *You have to find a place inside you, around you. A place that's right for you.*

A place that resembles you, at least in part.

His mother resembles the sea, the same liquid glance, the same calm hiding a tempest inside.

She never goes down to the sea except sometimes at sunset, when the sun sliding past the horizon reddens the rocks to purple and the sky to blood, and seems truly like the last sun on earth.

Vito watched Angelina walk along the rocks, her hair

unravelled by the wind, a spent cigarette in her hand. Scrambling along the cliff like a crab with the tide. It was just a passing moment, but he worried he'd never see her again.

His mother was Arab for eleven years.

She looks at the sea like the Arabs, as if she were looking at a blade, the blood already dripping.

Nonna Santa landed in Libya with the colonists in 1938. She was the seventh of nine children. Her father and her uncles made pottery. They set sail from Genoa beneath a pounding rain. The sky was filled with sodden handkerchiefs bidding farewell to the colonists of the Fourth Shore.

Nonno Antonio arrived on the last ship, the one that set sail from Sicily with sacks of seeds, vine shoots, bunches of chilli peppers. He was a thin little boy with olive skin. His hat was bigger than his face. He had never crossed the sea. He lived inland, at the foot of Mount Etna. His parents were farmers. They slept on their sacks. Antonio vomited out his soul. When they disembarked, he was deathly pale, but he perked up the second he got a whiff of the air. Mingled smells – coffee, mint, perfumed sweets. Not even the camels in the military parade stank. Vito must have heard Nonno

Antonio's story about landing in Tripoli thousands of times, about Italo Balbo in his hydroplane leading the way, about the immense tri-coloured flag spread out upon the beach and Mussolini astride his horse, the sword of Islam raised in his hand, pointing towards Italy.

His family spent a day seeing the sights of Tripoli and then they were taken to the rural villages. They found themselves face to face with kilometres of desert. Shrubs were the only vegetation. They set to work. Many of the Italians were Jewish.

They befriended the Arabs. They taught them agricultural techniques. They were poor people with other poor people. Their foreheads bore the same furrows of land and exertion. They cooked unleavened bread on hot stones, dry-cured their olives with salt. They dug wells, built walls to defend the cultivated land from the desert wind.

Santa and Antonio's families ended up on neighbouring farms. They helped their parents with the farm work, saw the citrus groves grow up out of the sand, learnt Arabic. They exchanged their first kiss in Benghazi during a Berber horseshow in Il Duce's honour.

Then war broke out. Friendly fire shot Italo Balbo down at Tobruk. A mistake, they said. English flares lit up the sky. The Italian colonists were sent back where they came from.

Antonio's family was transported back to Italy on the

cruise ship *Conte Rosso*, which British torpedoes sank when it returned to Libya.

After the war, many Italians went back to Libya on whatever boats they could find, rotten and overburdened fishing boats, Noah's arks like today's boats full of unfortunates. A reverse crossing of mare nostrum to regain homes, years of toil, cultivated fields. Or simply for love, like the seventeen-year-old Antonio.

He stowed away in the hold of a fishing boat from Marsala, buried like a dead fish beneath stinking nets. He disembarked, deathly pale, in Tripoli, where Santa's family now lived because her father was one of the workers on the city's sewer system.

The Tripolini welcomed the sea survivors like long-lost brothers. They disliked the English. The Italians were black from the sun, spoke some Arabic, drank mint tea on rugs at sunset. They had crammed themselves into the same narrow lanes. They were survivors, like them. They were clever, driven.

Then, in the 1950s, the Italians hit luck. They had children, opened restaurants, small factories, construction firms. They cultivated kilometres of sand.

Antonio was short, with hollow cheeks and pigeon-breasted from generations of malnourishment. Santa was robust. Her head brushed the ceiling. Dark, with green eyes and a double mole that seemed to move upon her face like an ant trying to climb. They were married in the cathedral. Antonio's jacket was as long as a coat. Santa wore a short veil. Two donkeys tricked out with bells and little mirrors that reflected the miraculous light of the sunset behind the medina pulled their Arab cart beneath the light posts and palms lining the promenade beside the Red Castle.

They expanded an old candle workshop. They lit up Christian holidays and death vigils in the mosques.

Once a week, Gazel the beekeeper came in his old Ford to deliver blocks of wax, crude and rubbery and dark as tobacco but golden as resin on the inside. Santa melted the blocks of wax beneath an almost invisible flame. As it boiled, she used a sieve to filter out impurities, greasy grey pieces of beehive that floated like leftover bits of placenta. She refined it until the yellow wax became colourless and odourless, the colour of silence, she said. Antonio prepared the mixes they used for dyeing, poured the wax into the moulds, scented it with cardamom and citrus fruit, and inserted the wicks. He tried everything, dropping rose petals into the still-wet wax, or fibrous hearts of palm. He passed a little studded roller back and forth across the wax to make patterned candles, spreading it like pasta dough, rolling the waxy sheets with his bare hands, his palms soft and numb to the heat.

They found a house in the Case Operaie quarter.

A boy came first, Vito, who died when he was just a few months old and was buried in Hammangi Cemetery.

The wax sheets hung like sore tongues in the dark, still workshop.

It was 1959, and all of a sudden oil gushed in Jebel Zelten. The 'Box of Sand' with nothing to export but battle scraps from the Second World War changed its wretched face. Now it was time for the war between the international oil companies.

In the meantime, Santa was pregnant again. She prayed in the Church of San Francesco. Every day at dawn, she pulled her most beautiful candle from the pocket of her work apron and lit it below the feet of the saint.

Angelina presented herself feet first. In Italy, she would have been born by caesarean. In Tripoli, she was born at home with a midwife whose arms were tinted with henna to the elbow. The midwife inserted a hand and performed the manoeuvre.

Angelina went to the Suore Bianche Nursery School, then to Roma Elementary School. Every morning she crossed the railway bridge. She ate fresh seeds in the souk, breathed in the burning-hot pepper smell of *filfil*. She raced on her bike to Piazza della Ghiacciaia, went swimming at the beach with the sulphur pools, waited for a glimpse of the Flying Angels, acrobats on motorcycles. Tripoli was simply her city. The songs of the muezzin punctuated her days. She knew she was foreign. *Taliana*. Her origins were something extra, an additional resource. One day, she might leave to go to university, but then she would come back. Her life was here, between the Arch of Marcus Aurelius and the mulberry tree, beneath the light that touched the ground and burnt with the red of the desert and the jubilant moula-moula birds.

Then came the Six Day War and pogroms against the Jews – dead bodies, burnt houses, the butcher slaughtered in front of his meat display.

Next came a fateful September day, a curfew, the city wrapped in a pall of subterfuge, suspended in silence.

Everyone thought King Idris had died.

He wasn't in the city. He was in Turkey for medical care. The old Senussi king had shown scarce commitment to the Arab cause. He was ceremonious with foreigners and had allowed the Americans to build a huge base for control of the Mediterranean. But he was praised and respected. Thin, inoffensive, with a long wizard's beard, he leant on his twisted stick.

In the candle workshop, Antonio sat glued to the radio.

He heard about the coup and its leader, a young man from the desert, handsome as an actor, seductive as a martyr.

Charismatic like his idol, Nasser of Egypt.

No bloodshed, only green flags. The people's revolution, they said. Even though there were very few of them, the Bedouin from Sirte and his twelve apostles, all very young.

It was the first day of the hunting season. Gazel the beekeeper had gone off after antelopes.

Angelina happened across his son, Alí, at Sciara Mizran. He was excited. There was a celebration in the streets. Huge tanks rolled along, peaceful, like big toys. They mixed in with the crowd and ran together to the sea, to the raft across from the castle. They swam for ages, an infinite swim. The water was so clear it was as if the bottom were a carpet and they were floating suspended on high, light as flying fish.

They stayed by the sea until sunset, their bodies close, their bathing suits drying on their bodies. They talked about the future. Alí always wanted to talk about the future. He was not much older than she, but that September afternoon, he already seemed like a man.

It started with the Jews.

The very Jews who had lived freely in Tripoli under Fascism, serving as colonial traders, drinking tea under tulle gazebos, dancing in private clubs – all despite the racial laws promulgated in Rome.

One day, Renata and Fiamma, Angelina's classmates, were not there for roll call.

The headmistress came. The teacher went out to the hall to cry.

Angelina looked at the map of Italy on the wall and at the palm trees outside the window. She looked at the two empty desks. She was eleven years old. It was the start of her first year of middle school. Her breasts were two swollen buttons. She wore white sandals and had started wearing perfume two months earlier.

Angelina did not know that she wouldn't finish the school year either. Soon, the school would close; the desks would be tossed in a heap, the alphabet and crucifix pulled from the wall.

She wouldn't see things like this again. The sea beyond the medina, the little mermaid fountain, the covered market, the Gaby Cinema. If she'd had a camera, it would have made sense to take pictures, like a tourist. Of her house. Of Sicilian *arancini* on a tray. Of the old men who played dominoes under the mulberry tree. Of her friend Alí dripping with sea, hands on hips, swimming mask on, snorkel clenched in his so-white teeth.

Angelina did not know that the young Gaddafi would banish even the dead from Hammangi Cemetery, that Italy would transport back thousands and thousands of soldiers who had died in Libya.

That her father and mother, their friends from the Oliveti Village, from Sciara Derna and Sciara Puccini, from Case Operaie – the people who had built the roads, the buildings, the drainage pits for the sewage system, the people who had turned the desert into a fruit bowl – would be the ones to pay for the misdeeds of the cruel and overreaching colonialism of Giolitti's liberal Italy and of the Fascist Fourth Shore.

The wax, an odourless dough the colour of silence, slides onto the ground and covers the floor of the emporium. The door hangs off its hinges. A stray cat from the port, dirty with fish, lets out a husky meow.

Santa and Antonio watch the sea, their daughter between them.

The palm trees on Corso Sicilia wave and bend to

one side. The ghibli will be here soon, bearing grey dust that leaves sand in your mouth, in your hair, in your fingers. They won't be there any more. Saying goodbye to your own life is easy. It's a leaden dawn. They're alive. That's what matters.

Vito looks at the sea, which is beginning to calm, to withdraw. It seems angry about this retreat. It pounds indolently on the cliffs, disorderly, its strength diminished. Last night's storm left the water murky. You can't see the bottom. Vito thinks of a club at dawn, the dirty carpet, the smell of smoke and sweat, the crushed sofas, the brimming ashtrays, the cigarette butts and broken glasses on the ground. He thinks of his eighteenth birthday party.

His friends got drunk, popped pills. He saw them dancing, out of it, swaying back and forth practically without moving, like a bunch of sick seaweed. Their feet glued to the ground, feverish.

None of them knows what they will make of their lives, apart from the ones whose parents own a business; a space would be made for them in a sales point.

Vito doesn't know what to do with his life, either.

Until recently, he hadn't even thought about it. He was laid-back. His thoughts were: go out, come up with

the money to go out, the money for petrol or for beer
and a kebab, pull one over on his mother, get someone
to dictate the homework to him over the phone, get a
ride on Saturday from someone with a licence so he
could go out to eat in Catania, go window-shopping in
Corso Italia, movies, the black prostitutes in Via di
Prima.

His eighteenth year brought bad luck. All of a sudden,
he started to think.

There, in that club that reminded him of a rubbish
dump for youth, for whole lives, he started to think. It
struck him as sad that there weren't any old people, just
kids. He thought of his nonna Santa, with her dark
clothes and white hair, her hands that were always clean,
always soaking along with the vegetables. A crazy
thought. At home, he never talked with anyone, and
now, all of a sudden, he would have liked to have his
grandmother there with him alongside the deaf DJ.

A girl was crying in a corner, so full of alcohol she
couldn't stand. She had heavy legs, high heels. Her
make-up, blacker than her hair, formed two highways
as it marched down her cheeks. And he started running
down those black lanes. How many times had his friends
passed other cars on the highway, engine racing round
the curves, the tarmac moving so quickly you couldn't
see, eyes red dots in the dark.

They had fun trying to blind themselves with cheap Chinese lasers. They yelled. They laughed. They smoked.

They could have crashed a hundred times. Ended up in the newspaper. One more car peeled open on the evening news like a can of tuna, their faces from their identity cards displayed below.

He pictured his hairless face on his identity card. The one he got when he was sixteen. His hair in a crest, that stupid expression. He still looked like a little kid.

He should take a new picture in the photo booth and get a new identity card. He was an adult now. He could leave home. He could go to jail.

No one went near the girl in the mottled dark of the club, and it didn't pass his mind to do so, either. She was uninviting. She didn't even seem sad. She was like a black fountain with no other reason to be except to sit there and cry. She didn't invoke pity. You had the feeling you could take her, pull her by a shoulder, and chuck her out of the club. With no change in expression, she would stop to cry beneath an oleander tree. She was one of those girls who'd go back home like that, to smear eyeliner onto the pillow from black, salty, bitter cheeks. Then take a shower, put on a maxipad, go to school, start moving once more, like seaweed. And then, when they happen across a couch in a club again, they start crying, just like that, with no reason, because they haven't ever stopped, because it's their way of communicating or of isolating themselves or of attracting attention. It doesn't really matter which. Like the other girl, the thin one who laughs. She just comes into a club and starts laughing. Maybe it's only because she has white teeth that glow phosphorescent in the play of light. Everyone dances. No one cares. Behaviours that travel, that pass from body to body. Attempts at life. Repeat as best you can the things you know how to do. Put emotions on display like a violent hailstorm. As if they aren't yours. You're just trying them on, dancing along to them with everyone else. You are just the face where the hail falls, where the strobe lights briefly linger.

Then, he doesn't remember how, he tongue-kissed that sweaty doughball. He sucked up that warm, swampy mess.

Vito looks at the blind, grainy horizon and at the beach, a dump of vomited objects. Now the sea looks like a pan lid, silver like a coin.

Back and forth across that stretch of sea, that's his family's history.

Angelina told him about their banishment, the guns pointed at them, how they were pushed along from behind. Their Arab life snatched away from them, the beach with the sulphur pools, the mulberry tree at Sciara Derna, the Roma Elementary School, their life-long friends.

All swept away one stormy morning.

A shattered life. That's his mother's story.

His mother knows what it means to face the sea from the other direction.

Like migratory birds.

Angelina told him birds know to leave their eggs in safe places. Our eggs were broken. Torn apart. Our houses stuffed inside a suitcase. We were snatched from our shell to run, to flee.

Behind them, a burning clothesline. Shirts, under-pants in flames. Soldiers with red caps among the eucalyptus plants, shouting, *Rumi!*, Italians, and spitting.

Angelina remembers one of them, the one who knocked over the barrel of boiling wax with his crossbar. Dark-complexioned but with blue eyes and hair so blond it almost looked like he'd dyed it. The son of a rape.

She didn't know anything about that violence. That came later, when she learnt about the rapes, when she saw the photographs of unmarked graves in the sand and of rows of hanging Bedouins.

Angelina was eleven in 1970. It was the start of her first year of middle school.

People shouting, lines outside the ministries and the consulate. Authorization to leave the country. A certificate of propertylessness. Everyone running with no clear destination, clinging to the walls like lizards, gathering news that changed each day. No one went into the medina any more. All the stores were shuttered. And there were two ugly men, one with wet purple lips, the other darker. Their Alfa Romeo drove slowly in the Italian areas, beneath houses and shops that in a short time would be expropriated.

Angelina remembers the night of the cholera vaccines. Clinging to her mother's dressing gown, to her candle-pale face. The colour of silence, for real.

Why did they give them that mandatory vaccine that came from Italy? What was the reason? They gave it to them without changing the syringe. Thank goodness there were no consequences.

When she told that story to her son, she showed him the exact place on her arm where the needle went in.

Vito took notes for his school-leaving research paper.

'I can't include everything, Ma.'

'Then why are you asking me so many questions?'

★   ★   ★

That night, Angelina learnt about war. She lost every boundary inhabited by trust. The feeling of emptiness, of plunder. If you took one wrong step, if you looked where you weren't supposed to, if your legs faltered even a bit. Beyond the line was the abyss. Uniformed Arabs scrutinizing your trembling.

Santa held her close, wrung her hand. Angelina's heart was beating like a drum. She was scared of that uncontrollable noise. It was so loud it seemed everyone could hear it. It wasn't a heart any more. It was a hammer pounding like the copper beaters in the market. The night around them was a black fire. Everything she had experienced as friendly and unspoken had turned into an ambush. The walls of prickly pears, the spires of the minarets. She thought about the massacre of Sciara Sciat. They'd just studied it at school. Italian *bersaglieri*, young as could be, plunged into the hubris of colonial conquest. They'd advanced quietly through the silent white city, calm as a manger scene. Tripoli had fallen effortlessly. The Arabs, it seemed, had been subdued and had retreated into the desert. The Turks were the real enemy. Then they heard sounds, mysterious as bird calls, and saw turbaned shadows, sure-footed as scorpions in the dark. An open front. No cover. The labyrinth of the oasis settlements on one side, the hot breath of the

Sahara on the other. Some of the *bersaglieri* sought refuge in the little Rebab Cemetery. Six hundred of them died, their throats slit, tortured and crucified like rag dolls. It was an October evening in 1911.

The Italian reprisals were terrible. The inhabitants of the Mechiya Oasis were dragged from their mud huts, the oasis villages torched. Thousands of summary executions. The survivors were exiled to the Tremiti Islands, to Ustica, to Ponza.

Now that hatred had sprung back to life.

That hatred was the revolution of the Bedouin from Sirte, whose body beneath his uniform bore scars from the mines of the colonial wars.

All around the city bonfires burnt European books by blasphemous writers, imperialist and corrupt.

Taliani murderers! Taliani out!

Angelina bared her arm for the vaccine. She didn't dare breathe. One drop of blood came out, one stupid drop of blood.

They left their house, the beds, the candle workshop. Antonio left the keys to the VW Bug in the glove compartment. He wanted to throw them in the sand but changed his mind. On holidays, that car had taken them to the archaeological site at Leptis Magna, where they ate sandwiches in front of the Medusa's head and went swimming.

They walked to the port. They waited for hours. They were searched and treated like criminals.

Angelina's Arab friends scratched their faces in sorrow, in the way customary to funerals. The kids she played with on the stone stretch in front of the candle workshop, hopscotch and grandmother's footsteps.

Ma sha' Allah. May God protect you.

Vito looks at the sea.

Angelina told him about the cushion she'd clutched as if it were a doll. An amaranth satin cushion with golden embroidery, a gift from her friend Alí, the thin boy, tall for his age, with his straight, shiny hair so black it was almost blue, parted on one side. When they went swimming, he'd take off his glasses and wrap them in his T-shirt. She'd wave her fingers in front of his eyes. *How many fingers do you see?* From a distance, Alí could hardly see and so always got it wrong. He'd get angry. He was a touchy kid. But he'd pretend it didn't matter. He'd plunge into the water, swim like a fish, hugging the bottom for so long she'd worry he was dead. She'd start looking for his head in the water, hoping he'd surface. Suddenly, Alí would emerge from the immobile sea. He'd push off with his feet from the bottom and jump out like a dolphin's spray.

The son of Gazel the beekeeper came with his father to the candle workshop, crouched on the ragged black seat of the red Ford with the wax and cages of hens and baskets of grapes. Alí always wore a striped cloth baseball cap and glasses with thick lenses, always carried a book in his hand.

Once they brought her to see the beehives, their first outing together. Angelina hopped into the Ford. They drove alongside the old Roman ruins as far as a Berber village. Alí gave Angelina a big metallic coverall and netting to cover her face, but he took off his glasses and his shirt and stood bare-chested, motionless, his arms spread wide like a Tuareg scarecrow, and let the bees cover him. The bees buzzed but had no apparent effect on Alí. There were so many of them that they formed a noisy pelt with every whisper of wind. Alí's eyes were immobile, fixed on her. They looked like the eyes of an animal invaded by smaller animals. They were haunted and incredibly sad. Or maybe he was just concentrating. Angelina opened a hand. *How many fingers do you see?* Alí couldn't speak, couldn't laugh. His mouth looked like a wound that had been pasted on. She continued to raise and lower her fingers. *Now how many?* It bothered her that he was so much better than her at everything, that he had such a stock of obstinate courage. Alí answered, *Six*, and guessed right. Maybe fear improved his vision. But a bee flew into his mouth and stung him in the throat. Angelina saw his dark, sad eyes redden and swell, become desperate. He seemed to be asking her for help with his entire being. He couldn't cough, couldn't move. But his throat was swelling up. He began to pant, to let out strange gasps as if about to lose consciousness. The bees were angry. Their buzzing grew louder and louder. Even if only half that colony of bees had decided to sting him, Alí would have died on the spot. He fell to his knees. Angelina backed away in terror.

Alí's father saved him by grabbing a hose and blasting him with a violent jet of water. The bees fell like shorn fur and formed a wet, hissing cloud on the sand. Alí was carried into the house and immersed in a soup of Yemenite herbs and ammonia powder.

He had a high fever. He was delirious.

He reappeared a week later.

He studied at the madrasa, where they wrote in notebooks but also on boards. Angelina went to wait for him outside, but he wouldn't look at her.

Angelina was sad. She had gone over that scene a

thousand times in her mind. She was the one who'd provoked him. She'd made faces at him. She was jealous of his courage, of the way he could stand still like a marabout. She wouldn't have lasted even a second. At night, she felt a stinger in her throat. She developed a nervous cough that scratched her tonsils whenever she thought of the danger they'd risked. She dreamt of Alí twisting and turning and dying on the sand, devoured by the bees. She dreamt of that thin body swollen with poison and bleeding from the stings.

Then Alí came back. One early summer afternoon, she saw him in the Italian gelateria Polo Nord. He was licking his ice cream, his eyes in their thick glasses fixed on a book.

'What are you reading?'

It was a collection of poetry by Ibn Hazm. He read her one. *I wish I could split myself in two with a knife, so that you could come inside and be enclosed within my chest . . .*

Beneath the cloth of his trousers, he touched the oyster knife he always carried. Alí was almost thirteen. There was a light fuzz beneath the sweat on his upper lip. Angelina looked at him, blushed. Alí was different. He'd never been shy and now he was, almost trembling, like the asphodel blooming at their backs. Everything was aquiver with a soft orange light that bore a suffering of its own within, as if some world behind them were retreating to another place.

It was childhood retreating before a new season of intimacy and shame. At the time, Angelina knew too little to interpret the sense of loss, the tragedy. It started raining. They ran off to their own houses. Angelina stopped to rest beneath the rubber tree.

She liked the rain in Tripoli. It was violent, sudden, like her emotions. Angelina let it soak her, her white sandals, her bare legs, her curly hair that was fairer at the ends. She could feel something inside, Alí's hand snatching her away from herself to introduce her into his Arab heart like in the poem.

The day they left, Alí ran to the white arch in front of Angelina's house. He waited for her a long time under the sun. Angelina was wearing her coat. He'd never seen her hair tied back so tight. Her father and mother were also wearing unseasonably heavy clothes. They'd put on everything they could. A form of protection. The weather had been interrupted; the seasons ahead were a jumble, confused like their layers of clothing. Alí thought they would sweat during their journey.

He would never again come with his father to deliver blocks of crude wax to the Italian candle workshop. His father wouldn't stay to drink the freshly squeezed juice of Sicilian oranges with Antonio or to play dominoes beneath the fig branches. He wouldn't wait again for Angelina's legs to come leaping down the stairs, for her pointed face, her cruel green eyes. When she emerged from the shadows, from the smell of wax and cardamom, one leg appearing through the crack in the door, she'd look at him as if he were a cockroach that only sheer laziness kept her from crushing. Alí didn't go into the candle workshop, just leant against the dusty body of the Ford, pretending to read.

Neither wanted to submit to the other.

When finally they'd start playing, it was already too late, already time for Alí and his father to go. They'd been stupid. He'd leave with an uncontainable wistfulness, a shout of injustice. They played together like no one else, as if they were one mouth singing, a single leg jumping. They were attuned to each other like birds on a single route. The same thoughts, the same movements.

The day Angelina left, Alí did enter the workshop. The door was half closed, everything flung about. The workshop with its spent and marshy aftertaste was like a desecrated church, the stiff wax stuck to the table, the cedar boxes tossed around higgledy-piggledy, the wax sheets hanging from the long wire, tattered like flags of a dead kingdom, like the flags of King Idris. A cat sat on the spent burners cleaning its tummy fur, paws open, tail in the air. Another drank from the stone water basin.

The family came out through the door, silent, compliant.

Santa and Antonio bid farewell to the beekeeper's son, kissed his cheeks.

The green door of the candle workshop hung unattended behind them. They looked like three different people. Three pallid masks lacking any expression connecting them to the life Alí had seen them live until that day. It was as if someone had killed them during the night, then made them again from wax, poured them into moulds of themselves. There was a certain resemblance, but they were no longer themselves. They were like stuffed birds, even their eyes were glassy and full of death.

They didn't seem to have the same feelings as before.

Angelina looked older. She was taller and shapelier in her dark wool coat buttoned to the neck. She moved stiffly, like a mechanical doll, as if someone had given her precise instructions.

She behaved exactly like a deportee, someone condemned to death for an unspeakable sin.

She looked like she was guilty of something. So did her parents.

Alí wanted to melt into warm tears in her arms. He trembled feverishly. He hadn't slept. He'd waited for her in the sun, beneath the rubber tree they'd scratched together so many times.

Angelina was rigid. She extended a hard, adult arm.

'Goodbye, Alí. Good luck.'

It was her mother who pushed them to kiss each other. She was the one who pushed her against him like a stone.

Alí gathered up his courage and thrust his gift into her arms.

It was a cushion, used but very elegant, made of dark red satin with a gold border. On top, he'd put some merguez, the dark little sausages she liked so much.

It was strange to see sausages on a satin pillow. Some kind of declaration of love.

Since he couldn't rip his heart out of his chest and give it to her, he'd made do with sausages. Angelina looked at them without moving a muscle.

Alí studied her from behind his glasses with his stupid face that would have liked to tell her all his plans. In a few years he'd be of legal age. He'd go to Italy, like his cousin Mohamed. They could get married. Because this was his father and mother's pillow, the bride and groom's pillow.

'It's very precious.'

It didn't seem so precious. The satin was old and worn, the fringe dark with age.

Angelina gave him a photograph, the best one she had, taken by the school photographer. She was in profile, looking out of a big glass window, bathed in a bleached light that made her look enigmatic. Alí stood looking at the photo with his diffident smile. What were a few years to a boy who could withstand an attack by hundreds of bees?

Angelina put the sausages in her pocket and the cushion inside her coat.

She looked like a little girl pregnant with an Arab cushion.

It kept her company during the long wait for the security check. A disabled boy was forced to get out of his wheelchair and was left hobbling around on his stumps like the lizards the Tuaregs roast in the desert.

Angelina was sucking on the fringe of Alí's cushion, squeezing it between her chattering teeth. The soldiers yelled at her to open her coat. They snatched away the cushion, gutted it with their bayonets. Who knew what they thought they'd find in a sweaty, saliva-damp pillow a scared girl had been sucking? Money, jewels, packets of drugs – who knew?

Small grey feathers filled the sea. The feathers travelled on the wind all the way to the castle where she and Alí liked to swim. There was a white grouper hiding somewhere in the fine, veil-like seaweed near the sandy bottom. Angelina waved to the fish from the ship, to the majestic palms of Corso Sicilia, to the Red Castle.

Angelina knows what it means to start over.

To turn and see nothing but the sea.

Your roots swallowed up by the sea, for no acceptable reason.

Angelina learnt to live with human irrationality. The mere appearance of the image of the dictator in his turban and sunglasses turned her into something alien, strange. What kind of face was that? That hair like inky spiders.

Angelina had been Arab for eleven years.

Adolescence was round the corner. It was a passage. A blow to the stomach.

There's something about the place where one is

born. Not everyone knows it. The ones who know it are those who are torn away by force.

An umbilical cord buried in the sand.

A sorrow that pulls from below and makes you hate the things you do afterwards.

You have lost your bearings, the star that followed you and that you followed in the radiance of those nights that were never entirely black.

For a time, Angelina no longer knew who she was. Someone gave her a label: Tripolina. A Tripolina from Tripoli.

They were all Tripolini, generations of rags tossed back from Libya to the place they'd come from.

Without anything any more, assigned to refugee camps in Campania, Puglia, places up north. Queuing up in front of the lavatories, toilet paper in hand. Slippers in the mud. Pasta in plastic trays. A television on a folding chair. A campsite full of pretend holidaymakers. A transit zone where life stood still.

Older refugees were incapable of thinking about starting over.

Angelina and her parents were lucky. They were sent to a seaside inn.

A basement dining room with greenish walls.

Sandwiches in bags. A mud-coloured cube of jam. Angelina's father folds his napkin into his plastic napkin holder. They are not paying guests. The waiter hollers at them to hurry. At night, she and her mother walk like two ghosts towards the shared bathroom.

Where was that inn? Some second-rate tourist destination, lifeless, with half-finished houses, a place where Mafiosi waited out their exile.

Santa ironing their clothes with a travel iron on the bed.

Antonio looking out onto the cement ramp of a garage. Cars going endlessly round the same curve.

His thin arms like broken wings in his short-sleeved shirt with its ironed-in pleats.

A row of lemons on the windowsill, their vitamin supply.

Angelina remembers the playground in the treeless park outside, the metal seesaw that wouldn't go up, pathetic with its two little seats. Angelina bent and straightened her legs like a frog. She needed another child on the other end.

She needed sand in her eyes, her hair. Where was the Gambrinus Café, the open-air cinema, the parties at Circolo Italia? Where were all their friends?

No one greeted them. They knew no one.

The smell of an incinerator, of burning rubber. They

went to bed with that smell. It seeped into their room. Their stock of perfumed candles ran out. They bought factory-made citronella candles. Santa said, *It's not real wax. It's full of junk.*

Her father said, *It's temporary.*

Then the State assigned them housing, Sicily at last. It was like the day of rebirth.

A black box. Windows that looked out onto a wall. In a port area, on the outskirts.

Her parents never got used to it. They sat in front of the television, eating sardines from the can. They didn't recognize anything, and no one recognized them.

Mute as statues made of sand.

Her father going out to find work. Angelina remembers her mother's gesture as she stood behind him, dusting off his shoulder, remembers the way Antonio turned. *What is it? Am I dirty?*

Santa accompanying him to the door. She stays there looking at the dark stairwell, at the stairs leading up. She breathes in the odours of the other lives inhabiting that crater, their sauces, their basements.

She's like a wary mouse waiting for the right moment to go out.

There were no human figures in that new life, only

shouting and vulgarity, and no one had any need of them.

Tripoli was full of beggars, old Berbers in filthy djellabas with missing buttons. There were black people, too, crippled, mutilated, escapees from some massacre or another. Santa wouldn't let them into the candle workshop, but she always gave them something: old clothes, a candle for the night.

Now Angelina and her parents are the poor ones. Poor white people, displaced, with the same discredited eyes as anyone who has lost.

They only raise their eyes from the ground when they need to seek confirmation of their existence in the other human bodies moving along the street.

It was the 1970s; the world around them was self-absorbed. No one cared about their diaspora. They were the dirty tail of a colonial history no one wanted to dig up.

That was the real exile, the moral solitude.

Antonio has his little black plastic pouch full of documents, made the worse for wear by queues and his hands that sweat when he speaks. He shows the paper that documents his status as a repatriated person.

The faces behind the windows look at him askance, ill at ease.

Why did you come back? To steal work from other Italians, from real Italians born and bred here? To move ahead of them on the unemployment lists?

When you came down to it, they'd asked for it. What did it matter that they were the children of peasants deported to Libya by propaganda, propelled by hunger?

Gaddafi reclaimed what was his. Italy was the guilty party, and they were leftovers from that guilt. A lesser species of unfortunates.

In the beginning, there was a committee. They kept in touch with the other exiled Italians. But then they stopped seeking anyone out. Everything unravelled.

They were alone, like monkeys burnt by boiling oil. Silently tending their wounds and sighing.

Santa gave up fighting. Somewhere inside, she started to feel guilty. To seem guilty. She couldn't get rid of that feeling of being lost, of diminishment. People deprived of themselves lose their boundaries. Put their back up against the wall and they'll confess to a murder they didn't commit. They certainly had not killed the Bedouins in the concentration camps. They had done nothing but work, make Libya beautiful, dig sewers and wells. They had poured and refined kilometres of wax blessed by bishops and imams.

★   ★   ★

Antonio had always been frail, his clothes hanging off him as if from a wooden silhouette. Now Santa seemed even frailer than he. She repeated things inside her silence. She thought about the dead baby alone in the Christian cemetery in Tripoli. They hadn't had time to take him with them, hadn't had the money for a bribe. She shook her head like a bird pecking from a branch that's too far away. She lost forty-five pounds in weight.

Angelina remembers a glimpse she caught of her mother's chest one day as Santa washed her underarms in the little sink beside the washing machine. Those imposing breasts reduced to empty sacks with little purplish tips.

They waited. For the repatriation compensation.

They talked of nothing but that compensation, which would put them back on their feet.

And their questions, repeated again and again. Why hadn't Aldo Moro accepted Gaddafi's invitation? Why had Italy underestimated the situation? There was a parliamentary crisis at the time, of course, but why should that have kept them from thinking about the Italians from Libya? People with first and last names and faces and their own beloved dead buried in cemeteries, all those children killed in the gastroenteritis epidemic.

Was this the way to repay the sacrifice of so many mothers?

It wasn't just about the money. They wanted to have back a name, a place. The compensation was for their dignity. The salty toil, the blood that had been shed.

So they could lift their chins and say, *Our country compensated us. We are victims of history*.

Years passed with that vain struggle. Because words lose their meaning if they are repeated too many times. Thoughts become a lethal gas.

It was the time of Red terrorism, Fascist terrorism, secret services.

The story of their exodus fell to tatters like a kite broken by a wind that blows too strong.

They had been reduced to the odd photograph, a little committee, pointless commemoration ceremonies. Already they had become a big banqueting hall of homesick refugees eating couscous in Brianza, in the Veneto.

Santa has trouble moving one of her arms. A pain nailed into her bones.

She sees a health service psychiatrist, who writes her

a prescription so she won't suffocate when she lies down at night. It's as if a hand is pressing on her sternum. Lead on her chest. All those coffins carried back by the Italian fighter jets and her little creature left in that desecrated place.

She can't come to terms with her anguish that those remains, remains of herself, of her uterus, were abandoned to that cemetery, where the graves left behind might have been desecrated out of religious vandalism or in order to steal a small coral necklace.

She dreams of little bits of beehive floating in wax.

Antonio's eyes looked like someone had smeared ointment over them.

He found work in the packing room of a factory that made office furniture. Then he moved to accounts. He was scrupulous. He checked his calculations late into the night until they came out right, a man obsessed.

After an injustice, you either go crazy or you hide.

Angelina remembers her church clothes from Christian charity. They smelled like other children, other closets. At first, she liked those packages her mother brought home, the skirts and coats matted by other little girls.

She'd smell the wool, flowing with other little lives like hers.

A stuffy smell of mothballs, of leftovers.

But soon enough, disgust set in. Like those black tides full of industrial waste in front of the buildings. She'd have preferred a rag from the market as long as it smelled of plastic, of new.

She was used to freedom, to endless warm weather, to the park with its majestic palms and large stone water basins, to the deep and inebriating smell of the souk, of roasted nuts, of fritters, of an infinite variety of coffee fragrances.

She stood out as rebellious, dishevelled. Her mother tried to make her like other girls, Italian girls born in Italy. Angelina looked around her. She, too, would have liked to have something or someone to resemble.

She looked for a fixed point in the sky. Perhaps an Arab star had followed her.

Outside her classroom windows, she no longer saw palm trees and colourful birds, just grey walls and cranes on construction sites for housing projects.

No one came near her at school. They all knew each other already. They looked at her bare legs. Angelina wore sandals until Christmas. Her feet were never cold.

No one knew anything about Tripoli. Even the teachers looked upon her as a foreigner from far away.

Her classmates called her the African. *You smell like a camel*, they said. The school was in an outlying neighbourhood of cheapened people who knew no way to approach others except poorly. Like different species in the savannah. The same circular walk of hyenas sliding, full of fear, towards their hunger. Angelina tried to adapt. She was excluded as a matter of course, without any real malice.

She made her alienation into an adventure.

She made things up, told stories about lions, children torn to pieces, baleful Tuaregs. Tripoli was a fearsome place and she had survived thanks to countless clever ploys. The stories earned her a bit of respect.

It was language that divided them. She didn't know Sicilian dialect, only the ornate Italian they taught at the Italian school in Tripoli.

She walked home alone. The stretch of road was truly long amongst all the cement and the stinking second-rate sea. Not a single whiff of asphodel or carob, not one friendly soul.

She thought about Alí. His heart. The oyster knife he carried in his pocket. One day, he'd join her. He'd marry her. They would go back to Tripoli. She could, if she married an Arab. Alí would be rich – he was smart and brave. He was thirteen years old and he'd already saved a nice little bundle of dinars. They'd buy the candle workshop. Her mother, standing before the doughy mixture the colour of silence, would start singing again.

Her father would twist candles again for Ramadan and for Christmas.

That was her one thought: how to bring her life back to that point.

The point where it had been interrupted.

It would mean uniting two bits of land, two bits of time.

The sea lay in the middle.

She lay split figs over her eyes to remember the flavour, sweet and lumpy. The seeds tinged all she saw with red. She was looking for the heart of the world she'd left behind.

Every time she went into the water she swam towards the open sea.

As she grew, she brought books with her to the black mineral beach.

She spent hours in the sea. She swam until she reached silence, where nothing and no one could get to her. She remembered how Alí swam, like a drowning seagull.

She looked back towards the beach, the industrial city without a sunset. It looked like a drawing of death, of the world after the end of the world. No voice, just billowing smokestacks.

She dived towards the depths, passing fearlessly

through stands of slimy funereal seaweed like buried arms. Her long blue flippers bore orange flame decorations. She thought she would swim to Tripoli. She'd end up half fish, half woman, like the mermaid in the legend. She'd linger near the city of carob trees and whitewashed walls and sing her secret song.

Vito looks at the sea, the island's beautiful sea, turquoise like in Africa. He looks at the coast with its mossy green inlets. They remind him of armrests on a big green velvet armchair set beside the water where a giant sits and surveys the horizon as he organizes the world and its movements.

Vito has thought more than once about the giant who organizes the world. He has wondered whether the giant is made of people, lots of people piled atop one another. And whether he'll be one of those tiny but fundamental people.

That's what a boy is supposed to want, to participate in the organization of the world. He's always been a fugitive, at school and elsewhere, a fugitive from any type of learning.

He lowers his head. He's ashamed of this sudden burst of ambition. He won't accomplish anything either good or remarkable. It's more likely his life will pass without notice. The sun flickers on the swampy, hot horizon. Vito feels the weight of his destiny moving slackly ahead of him in that swamp. He should seize it, shouldn't he? Take a leap. But how do you know which destiny awaits you? No one had an envelope with the answer to give you.

Why doesn't he jump into the sea for a swim?

This year he doesn't feel like it.

His mother has told him about her endless swims as a teenager. The sea was the only friendly place, the only place with a familiar taste and smell.

She says the sea saved her. It could have killed her, because more than once she swam until dark, unsparing of herself, and then had to swim back to shore through the black sea, her body shaking with hypothermia, shivering so hard ten blankets wouldn't stop it.

But without the sea she really wouldn't have known where to go to digest all that emptiness.

Vito looks at the sea.

His mother doesn't even get wet any more. Now and then she'll float a bit. Then she comes back out in her one-piece bathing suit, her towel round her waist.

That's all she does, floats like a dead person looking at the sky. She says she thinks and feels the surface stretching beneath her. She says it's a good feeling.

★   ★   ★

She adapted to the new world. She went to high school, made love for the first time. She got an IUD coil and forgot about Alí and her Arab childhood. It was the end of the 1970s. She wore the shabby uniform of that turbulent time: a loose sweater, black clogs, a macramé bag full of books, the woman symbol on her forehead. During the student demonstrations, her hands clenched into fists, she shouted like mad, her face that of a banished monkey's. At last, her rage found its audience in an entire generation of kids.

She couldn't stand her parents' exile any more, the constant stream of memories of Tripoli. The world was moving on, and she would do her part to make it better. There were social injustices, workplace fatalities, massacres of innocents the world over. Her family's wound was not the only one.

She created a wall for herself.

She could no longer stand the smell of their household, choking on nostalgia. Defeated people ceaselessly lamenting what had been snatched away. Her father clipped every article on Libya, on the story of their downfall.

They had relatives in Catania whom they'd visit a couple of times a year. Angelina made friends with her cousins. Santa and Antonio smiled and ate their lemon cassata, but they were like two deportees. They sat side by side and went through the motion of talking about other things, but they weren't really interested, and they ended up silent, her mother with her handbag in her lap, her father fiddling with the ten-lira coins in his pocket. They couldn't wait to leave.

They wanted to go back to their exile, where they were free to complain, to wallow in eternal sorrow.

Angelina began to flee, to slam the door.

She studied, too. She knew the true story of Italian colonialism now. Her family had been deported, exported, along with the Roman colonies, the Fascist eagles, the flames of a dying empire.

Antonio was a moderate. He voted for La Malfa's Republicans.

But there had been an antecedent. They had left more behind them than fine-grained sand and infinitely pure landscapes of dunes and oases.

There had been kangaroo courts, planes that landed in the desert and killed Libyans in bunches after hasty trials. Once, *Avanti!* printed a picture of a Christmas tree, Bedouins hanging from its branches instead of ornaments and garlands.

Vito looks at the sea.

His mother once told him that beneath every Western civilization lay a festering wound of collective guilt.

His mother isn't fond of people who protest their innocence.

She's one of those people who wants to assume responsibility for things. Vito thinks it's a form of presumptuousness.

Angelina says she's not innocent. She says that no people that has colonized another is innocent.

She says she doesn't want to swim any more in a sea where boats full of migrants sink.

There's nothing worse than an old revolutionary. She's always planting bombs in your thoughts.

There's nothing worse than having an unconventional mother. A mother who resembles no other mother, who wears beach sandals everywhere, whose handbag has nothing in it, cigarettes, house keys, ten euros, a mobile phone she never uses. A handbag without miracles. Like her life.

One day, Vito will leave her. The two of them have lived alone. If there was a light on in the house, it was her, no one else. The books propped open on the couch. Like an eternal student. She's shrunk since she turned fifty. He's the one who tells her to stand up straight, not to slouch. He's the one who tells her not to smoke.

She just shakes her head and says Falcone and Borsellino smoked, too, and that's not what killed them.

She's always saying things like that, absurd things that carry on speaking in the silence.

That illustrate her worldview, bitter but alive.

One day, he will leave her. She doesn't seem to be afraid of that day. If anything, she'd like him to go and study abroad.

She doesn't like Italy any more. But she goes on teaching Italian to middle-school kids without ever taking sick leave, not even for a day.

Her former students come to see her, hug her, drown atop her. She makes coffee for them and looks at them, all grown up.

When he was little, Vito would get seasick when they were crossing to the island. He'd go greenish. Angelina would hold his forehead with one of her hands, which were always cool to the touch. She'd tell him to find a still spot on the horizon and keep his eyes on it.

If he thinks about it, Vito can feel that discomfort all over again, his stomach heaving and dumping itself out like a plastic bag tossed around by the undertow. He can still feel that cool hand supporting him and pointing out the distant spot to look at.

He looks for a still spot on the horizon.

Something that will help him get through the despair that rises now out of nowhere in the morning. He opens his eyes and his first thought is, Why should I get out of bed?

Vito looks at the sea. As if he were casting a net to land and bring something back. He thinks about his mother. She's had breast cancer. She had an operation and came back home as if nothing had happened. Her face never changed. Vito wasn't kind. He was rude. He grabbed the packet of cigarettes away from her and tore it up. Angelina bit his hand.

Who does she think she is?

Then Angelina's sea closed.

She married, a Norman Sicilian, blond and freckled, an expert in civil law who defended hookers and juvenile delinquents from the blighted San Berillo neighbourhood. Angelina got a job as a substitute teacher. Vito was born. Angelina separated from Vito's father. Now her ex-husband helps Catania's wealthy to divorce well.

Then one day, out of nowhere, the ban was lifted. They could go back to Tripoli if they wanted to on a plain old tourist visa.

The Day of Revenge, 7 October, which commemorated the banishment of the Italian assassins by the colonel's Jamahiriya, was transformed overnight into the Day of Friendship. Gaddafi was now a friend of Berlusconi and of Italy. He came to visit with his Amazon Guard and his satin slippers. Champagne in the Bedouins' tent. No one said another thing about terrorism, exploded planes. His had been the first Arab government to condemn the attack on the World Trade Center. The actor of a thousand faces was now after a new role as mediator in the Mediterranean. Angelina laughed. *He's hoping for the Nobel Peace Prize.*

Nonna Santa, cleaning broccoli, whispers, *History is a millipede with every foot pulling in a different direction, and our body is in the middle.*

By then Nonno Antonio had already died without ever seeing Tripoli again. But he'd dreamt it, dreamt a white wall and the café in Corso Sicilia where he used to play pool. He'd ordered a cup of mint tea, the pretend kind from the supermarket.

'Mum, I want to go.'

It was Vito who dragged her back to Tripoli.

He was sick of hearing that broken story.

So Angelina and her mother travelled back with Vito, who'd never been.

Beforehand, he took a tour with Google Earth, saw Tripoli thanks to his mouse.

Angelina wouldn't come near the computer.

She went around with that expression for days, hunched into her shoulders, absent, paralysed by her thoughts.

She was anxious, caged in. She put things in her handbag and took them back out. She talked about nothing but what weather they would find and the intestinal antibacterial they'd better bring along in case they got the runs.

She'd waited for this moment for who knew how long, and now that it was here she seemed uninterested, cursory, like a person who finally has to go through a small but necessary operation she's put off many times. Yes, it was the same agitated calm as when she went to the hospital to get the lump in her breast removed and sat on the stretcher fully clothed, not making up her mind to change, to put on her hospital gown, until the very last minute.

That very same almost autistic determination, that habit of fighting against herself, of never choosing a new wall to scale.

In the end, she shuffled off in her slippers as if she were headed to the beach for a day.

Nonna Santa was like a little girl on Saint Agatha's

Day in her white dress and new orthopaedic shoes.

They flew on Libyan Airlines.

Nonna looked out of the dirty window and studied what she saw.

It was the first time they'd seen *that* sea from the air. Without the flavour, the foam spray, the anguish. Without the fear they'd drown.

It was a strange interlude within that pressurized cabin as it crossed the sea of their lives without moving.

The first thing they saw from above were the fields the Italians had created in the desert around Tripoli, a geometry of tidy pieces. A docile pattern. That was the best bequest, the work of thousands of arms. Citrus and olive groves, rows of agave planted as bulwarks against the mobile horizon of dunes.

They had no baggage and yet it was as if they didn't want to leave the airport. They closed themselves in the toilets. Nonna had a swollen bladder. Vito's mother rinsed her face, and when they came out, she had wet spots on her T-shirt and her hair was glued to her temples.

Vito noticed she'd grown old. The thought pained him. Later, she'd go back to being young, but in that moment, he saw what she would become.

★　　★　　★

The air of that sea, those cities unfurling themselves along the Arab coast, flat, caressed by the wind going in and out. Needle-like minarets, buildings surrounded by majestic palm trees. Vito was happy to be on holiday. They took a taxi. The country's oil wealth was tangible. Tarmac roads with multiple lanes sliced through the desert. Sparkling Toyotas drove arrogantly, making U-turns and nonchalantly cutting through roundabouts in the wrong direction.

The taxi stopped along the seaside promenade.

Nonna Santa straightened her neck, made a dizzy face, stretched like a grey bird. Her daughter helped her up from the sweaty car seat.

The two of them looked like they'd just stepped off a spaceship. The first steps they took were weightless, as if they feared setting down their feet.

Angelina lit a cigarette and put on her dark glasses. Her eyes darted here and there, taking everything in as quickly as a pickpocketing. Then she began moving forwards. Like a mine remover in the desert.

Her motionless eyes sought to catch everything possible in her visual field. Violently they brought all the changes into focus to avoid being wounded too much.

New buildings surrounding the old medina. Dusty old roads that had been paved over. The conference centre had not changed. Nostrils stretched wide as they breathed in Tripoli's smell. Sniffing after that eaten-up time as if checking for a gas leak. And it really did seem like something might explode. Angelina turned towards the sea.

The sand . . . where is the sand?

Their beach near the castle was no longer there. The promenade was an immense car park.

All of a sudden, she burst out laughing, like a crazy lady.

A cat rubbed up against her. A wary and absent creature, just like her, with flea-bitten ears and reddish fur. It tickled her leg. It was one of those soft cats, maybe in heat, that turn over and let you touch them. It lay there on the ground, four legs in the air, rubbing against the tarmac. Angelina bent over to pet its white belly. The cat purred. Angelina picked up the animal and kissed it on the nose as if it were a baby fresh from its bath. She didn't seem to want to leave the cat. Vito smiled. He liked animals, too, but there was something odd about his mother's sudden passion for the stray, as if she'd come all the way to Tripoli to find this sick and wounded cat. When she stood up, though, Angelina looked like something had healed her. She pushed her sunglasses back on her head and looked at the city with naked eyes. Then she looked at Santa.

Mum, do you remember all those cats when we left?

Nonna walked the entire length of Corso Sicilia without saying a word, unsteady on her feet. She sat on the pavement under a palm tree and Vito thought, There she is sitting at the end of her life. She took a deep breath. A hard, satisfied breath like a blade slicing in and reaching a vital organ.

Many of the buildings in the city centre were intact, though smaller and dirtier than they remembered. Others had literally been erased, submerged by layers of architecture, of lives. The old Jewish cemetery had disappeared, buried by extravagant, accordion-shaped skyscrapers set upon cement stilts.

Let's get an ice cream. A lemonade.

His mother took his grandmother's gnarled hand, and it was like looking forty years back in time, when Nonna would have been the one dragging little Angelina towards the cathedral, towards the Italian gelateria Polo Nord.

The streets were a jumble of cars, bikes, street

vendors. But they moved in a tight pattern. The two women were happier now. Two gun dogs looking for the scent, the right trace of blood. Their heads raised, they blocked out the noises of the city, the new bank buildings and conference centres. They were looking for their city, closed up too long. They scrambled through the narrow lanes and passageways of an interior topography. The stores had remained pretty drab, old mannequins in out-of-date clothes. In the market, beside the camel-hair bags, they saw piles of fake Louis Vuittons. The colonel's image graced every corner.

A year earlier, Vito had travelled to New York with his father. An all-male trip, the two of them and Vito's father's new son, who, unlike Vito, was fat and always wanting to eat and drink and suck on something. But he played the violin in a pretty miraculous way. They'd slept in a room with three beds with a view of the Hudson. One of those short and constantly excited holidays, always taking pictures of things before actually seeing them.

Vito wanted to go to Ground Zero. It was what interested him most. Like everyone, he remembered exactly where he was on that September day. He was alone with Nonna. His mother had a meeting at school.

His parents had just separated. He thought it was the end of the world. He waited by the window for the plane that would crash into their building.

At Ground Zero, he stayed watching the immense black space of the construction site. There were hordes of tourists glued to the security fences, taking pictures and talking.

Vito didn't reach for his mobile phone, didn't even make the gesture. He had imagined this crater in the city, but seeing it was different.

It really was the end of the world. Everything had been cleaned up. Years had passed. And yet it was all right here in this immense, empty black space.

Vito had seen the stories on TV, the people trying to recognize a flying body from a still frame. A man eternally frozen, head down in mid-air.

His father's kid wouldn't shut up. OK, he was his brother, but only half. He lived with another mother, and they had a lot more money.

He felt incredibly alone.

Like that day when his parents were the two towers that fell.

He suppressed his bad mood. They went to Central Park, walked round the lake. He couldn't shake the image of the big burnt lake a few blocks away. That night when they went to eat at Joe Allen, he didn't want to play superheroes on the table with his brother. His father got angry with him, and he got angry back. He spent the entire night looking out at the skyline with the two towers chopped out, the laptop glued to his knees. Once upon a time, he'd had a family. Now, he had only uncertainty and the money his father gave him every now and then, to buy an iPod or some clothes. He fantasized about breaking the glass that reached down to the street and jumping out, but it was probably shatterproof.

In Tripoli, he realized that the sensation had stuck with him, the burnt stink of his Ground Zero. Because out of nowhere, as he looked down an alley that smelled of coffee and pungent spices, which may have reminded him of the multiethnic stink of New York, he noticed a sense of panic that came and went. Just like cigarette smoke dissipating after someone blows it out.

Tripoli was their zero level, their memory razed to the ground, liquefied.

His father said Angelina was still a deportee. A person waiting for return. And that the marriage itself had been a sentence of internal exile.

His father is cut from a pattern just like his lawyerly jackets, always slipping away behind a river of words that watered down life, diluting it until it lost its bite. His mother is the exact opposite. The only thing she can be is herself. She doesn't dress up. She doesn't even wear a bra. Now Vito understands his father's divorce. Sometimes he feels like he's been taken in himself. Angelina is capable of saying nothing for days on end. She doesn't reproach him. She just does everything in silence, like Gandhi. She leaves notes. She was born to be an old maid. A solitary climber.

Once, in one of those notes, she'd written, *Break the emotional wall.* Was this meant for him, or herself? Vito crumpled it up like the others.

During those days in Tripoli, Vito understood a lot about her and her *mal d'afrique.* That minor affliction, fleeting, consisting of attacks that came and went like malarial fever, and her eyes afterwards, at once opaque and wounded, her sore tongue incapable of speech. As if she'd been bitten from the inside by a hidden animal. Now the animal was out in the open, sumptuous, voracious.

Vito watches his mother. Her hips and stomach move differently here, as if she's absorbed the rhythm of the sea, the waves with their long tendrils, the boy playing the oud beside the Fountain of the Gazelle. She's even taken off her beach sandals, which dangle from her hand, and her heels are turning black as if that were something to be proud of.

She's performed a biopsy of the city. She's analysed the unpleasant things that have replaced the beautiful missing things, and now she's enjoying the mutilation. Like when she recovered from cancer.

Nonna moved along like a zombie in the calvary of their return, all the more intense because it was so sudden. Angelina kept her going.

They poured themselves into that sifter of memories, at first fearful and then nearly crazed, hovering between anger and joy. Hair mussed, eyes flickering, a mirror of the fear of all the time that had passed, all the hunger. All the fishing boats that reached their destination and the ones that went down in the storms. Berber eyes, really. Eyes that dug into the depths of things that had been stolen and never returned.

Nonna grew more and more daring. She didn't have arthritis pains any more. She was agile and clever. She nosed her way into a mezzanine beneath the Ottoman arcades. *This is where Ahmed and Concetta had their kitchen.*

Do you remember? That focaccia with custard and aubergine ... the vine leaves stuffed with spicy meat. Next came the old Fascist buildings ... *And the barber was here. Do you remember? You used to ride horses with his daughter ...*

The Church of the Madonna della Guardia was now a gym, the cathedral a mosque. Piazza Castello and Piazza Italia had been joined to make the colonel's immense Green Square.

They crossed the railway bridge towards the Case Operaie quarter.

Their old neighbourhood was unrecognizable. The new had paved over the old. It was difficult to get their bearings. They found a metal-framed building where the house should have been. The candle workshop had also been buried somewhere. Nonna went around in a trance, murmuring to the stones like a diviner questioning the earth.

Vito thought again of Ground Zero. Of what would rise there. Of the fact that a day would come when no one would think about it any more.

Later, they got to Hammangi Cemetery. Rubbish bags and abandoned bed frames languished beneath the sun.

Now, the new foreigners were buried here – Chinese, Egyptians. The old Christian cemetery had come back to life. The Italian area was like a construction site. Entire walls had been emptied of remains once harboured in individual recesses, shelf after shelf like an empty library. They passed the abandoned tombs of unknown Italian soldiers and Italo Balbo's marble mausoleum, empty now too.

They came to the children's section. All the children who died during the gastroenteritis epidemic and others.

Nonna Santa went looking for her baby, dead fifty years earlier. She put on her glasses and climbed the ladder to see the names up high. She stuck her head into every gap, rummaging around the remains as if it were something she did every day, like at the market when she chose fruit and vegetables by moving boxes and rummaging beneath the top layer. As if it were something she was accustomed to, when instead it was so unreal. Dirty holes where mice had left their tracks. The richest families had managed to repatriate the remains of their loved ones, but their family hadn't had the money to insist on anything. But now, in her old age, Nonna Santa no longer remembered things in quite the same way. She'd rearranged her Libyan memories. Now, she said it was a blessing they'd left little Vito's remains in Tripoli, where he'd been born and lived his short time.

Vito was restless. A hard burp rose and stung his throat. He was hopeful for his grandmother, but personally anxious about the prospect of reading his own name on a tomb. Angelina wandered around across the aisle from them. Her memories did not coincide with her mother's. She stopped, angry.

What are you doing? Not there! Nonna was yelling.

She started fighting with her daughter. They had an absurd argument in the cemetery. They hollered at each other as if they were at the market. They threw rotten old things in each other's faces. It was almost comical. They were exhausted. It ended the way it usually did. Angelina took her mother's arm in her own, held back the tide.

The Christian cemetery had been vandalized repeatedly, human remains used in gruesome rituals. They searched until dark. In one part of the cemetery stood a big tree whose roots had grown into the graves. Maybe the baby had nourished that ancient plant. It was the most comforting thought they were able to muster.

Then his grandmother wept. Her elderly face began to tremble, and it seemed it would never be dry again. It was a terrible scene for Vito. He thought it was incredibly unfair to see an old person cry. More unfair than anything in the world.

She'd brought a bunch of sunflowers, which had wilted during their search. She didn't know what to do with them. She bent to set them down in a corner, a tuft of yellowish eyes that looked like they'd been plucked from shabby stuffed animals.

Before going back to their hotel, they wandered around the souk. Copper artisans, red henna, black dates, spices. Now they really were torn and wandering souls. Angelina, tinted blue by the veil she'd bought to go into Dorghut Mosque, allowed the crowd to drag her along, beat her like a rag.

Only then did Vito understand what his nonno had meant when he said, *The story of man is the story of hunger.* Hungry people moving around. The hunger of the poor, colonists, refugees. And the greedy hunger of the powerful.

Vito stuffed himself with spicy couscous.

The next day, they enlisted a guide. Namek was a university student who seemed a lot younger than his twenty-two years. He was a diversion for Vito, someone to whom he could talk. Namek was nice and a little crazy. He was mad about art and rock climbing. They set off to see Berber villages and archaeological digs, Leptis Magna and the sea.

They passed the rural Italian settlements. Porticoes that opened wide onto nothing, buildings marked with red for demolition, a defunct train station. Nonna said, *Who compensates you for what's been stolen? We had olive groves and friends. We had a history.*

It wasn't until they were about to leave that his mother started looking for Alí. She found the rubber tree where they used to meet. It had been reduced to a crooked old trunk, sick with dark, hard lumps. On the edge of the city, she found the old house with its powdery bricks.

There was no trace of the beehives and the rest. The place was abandoned. One door, its boards rotted and ragged and needlessly blocked with a rusty bolt. They caught a glimpse of the interior, dark as a barn. Some tiles were missing from the cracked walls. Splotches of light filtered through. Prickly pears had grown up everywhere, and the sagging roof had become a shelter for birds.

Some kids were playing football in a sandy patch of land. An old woman wrapped in a woollen shawl sat on a car seat in the parched field packaging up gunpowder for the festival of Mawlid, the Prophet's birthday. Angelina stopped to question her.

It was the first time Vito had heard his mother speak Arabic. Her voice sounded different, as if it were coming out of some other throat. The old woman shook her head. Gazel, the old beekeeper, had died a while back. Alí lived in the centre, in the special area.

Namek brought them to the building in the old Jewish quarter of Tripoli but refused to follow them under the arches and up the stairs. He shook his head and said he would wait for them at the bar with the big awning behind the clock tower.

There was a metal eyehole on the dark door. They heard someone stirring on the inside and realized they were being watched. Angelina coughed and rearranged her hair, her eyes on the spyhole. Then the door opened and a voice emerged from behind a tip of nose they glimpsed between the door and the wall, in the little space permitted by the door chain.

A massive woman let them in. It looked like she'd hurriedly tossed her rumpled veil over her head. She led them to a large room with high painted ceilings. Two big French doors, half closed, overlooked the street from one side of the room. The wail of the muezzin calling noon-day prayer arrived from the mosque next door. Vulgar modern furniture clashed with its surroundings. Shiny furniture, leather sofas with enormous armrests.

Vito and his mother were invited to sit. A younger

woman brought a tray with colourful carbonated beverages. Fake orangeade, fake Coca-Cola.

They waited about an hour, watching the dark screen of an immense plasma television on a little glass table beside a decorative plant. Every now and then, children of varying ages peeked through the door, but they never crossed the threshold.

At last, Alí arrived. He was elegantly dressed but didn't seem to have come in from outside, and Vito couldn't understand why he'd made them wait so long. He was handsome, tall, and without a bit of fat. He had a thick head of hair and a big black moustache beneath his glasses. He was wearing a bush jacket and copper-coloured summer-weight loafers.

He held out his hand to Angelina.

He didn't sit on the couches with them but on a chair with a tall, rigid back, crossing his long, thin legs.

His Italian was good.

He had a polite but firm manner. Two hard wrinkles cut through his hollow cheeks. Melancholy tinged his dark, persuasive voice. At a certain point, he said something in Arabic that Vito did not understand, a mysterious call.

Vito saw his mother shrink on the couch. She couldn't find a comfortable way to sit, couldn't avoid sinking in too deep, had to maintain the awkward position.

Alí was no longer tapping his fingers like a drum; he was looking Angelina right in the eyes. They were remembering old times, diving off the raft at the castle.

Angelina didn't ask him why he hadn't kept his promise. After all, she'd forgotten about him, too.

But perhaps never entirely.

That's what Vito thought, looking at her.

He grew irritated. He thought that if Gaddafi had let them grow up on the same shore, he would never have been born and his mother, her eyes rimmed with kohl, would have gone off in a mud-coloured jeep through the desert oil rigs and skyscrapers beside this leather-skinned Arab.

He wore a strong cologne, sandalwood and something else. Vito didn't like it.

He must be really rich. There was a strange atmosphere in the house, perhaps because not much light filtered in. It was like some kind of mausoleum.

When they remembered the bee episode, Alí stood, spread his arms like he'd done back then, like a scarecrow in the desert.

Angelina smiled, pulled out a hand.

'How many fingers?'

Alí smiled, too, but ruefully. He said that he had good glasses now, with varifocal lenses.

He took off his glasses, rubbed the dark circles sunken into the bones of his skull. He looked at Angelina.

'I can no longer permit myself not to be far-sighted.'

He had affable manners, long, polite fingers. He crossed his legs absent-mindedly, one foot in its heelless copper-coloured loafer.

But his eyes were still and penetrating. They resembled the static house, without a breath of air, like a bunker.

It was lunchtime. The two women served a big common bowl of *shorba*. The fat woman was the first wife, the younger woman the second. She wore a rather ugly Western-style blue dress and a diamond ring as big as a rock. She smoked a lot of cigarettes. She seemed sadder than the veiled fatty, who had clever eyes, curious about everything. When she passed in front of her husband, she made a slight bow.

Angelina didn't ask anything about them, just looked.

Alí said his second wife was Egyptian.

'She doesn't like being stuck in the house. She'd like to travel, but I am too busy.'

Angelina said she had divorced but that she didn't have other husbands around. Alí smiled. There was a long pause.

'Do you still read poetry?'

Alí didn't answer right away. He nodded and said he read a lot, but only politics. He worked for the State. He was a servant of Libya. His life was dedicated to his country.

Angelina looked around the room, the floors with their hand-painted bricks, the long windows giving onto the balcony.

'I think I might have been here before.'

Now Alí was lost in thought. Maybe he was growing tired of their visit. His eyes were like two dead insects beneath the glass of his lenses.

He insisted they try spoonfuls of a strange honey.

Angelina asked if it was his, from his hives. She thought he'd become a honey producer. Alí shook his head.

'It's bitter honey from Cyrenaica.'

He gave Vito a long look.

'Do you like it?'

Vito didn't like it.

Alí's face hardened. He smiled. One of his molars was gold.

'Our colonel's ancestors died in the Italian concentration camps in Cyrenaica. Did you know that?'

He rose, said he had to be going.

Shukran. Thank you.

He saw them out.

Only later, back on the street, did Angelina remember that Italians had lived in that building. That it might have been the home of Renata, her Jewish friend from Padua.

The waiter served mint tea, lifting the spout of the teapot upwards from the tiny cups with a practised, ample gesture. Angelina quizzed Namek about Alí. Their young guide looked around as if someone might arrest him at any moment. He was afraid of an 'antenna', a spy. A light sea breeze buffeted the deserted square. Namek knew Alí well. He was a bigwig in the Mukhabarat, Gaddafi's secret service. Namek was familiar with Alí's brigade. They ran at full speed through the streets, terrorizing people. They took dissidents from their houses at dawn. Every so often traitors would be displayed on television and interrogated. It was a way of intimidating people. During the adverts, the dissidents were beaten. You could see their eyes grow sadder and sadder, ever more distant. They had to confess, name names. Then they were brought to Abu Salim Prison, or else buried alive in holes beneath the sand outside the city. Namek was a Berber. Many of his relatives had been targeted. The colonel hated Berbers. They weren't allowed to speak their language or use their alphabet. Many never returned. Tortured, forced to repeat, *I'm a disgusting rat. Long live Muammar. Long live Muammar*, until they went mad. Young women raped by drunken militiamen who travelled with supplies of condoms and Viagra in the pockets of their uniforms.

Angelina rose and disappeared.

When she came back to their table, her face looked crooked, as if she'd banged into something that had left a mark.

Vito thought about that note in the kitchen: *Break the emotional wall.*

What lay beyond that wall?

Morning Sea

Farid is curled up against his mother on the boat. He isn't complaining any more. He's dehydrated. His legs are full of ants, like the ones that used to climb up his arms and make him laugh. Now they're inside him. Are these the footsteps of history?

Jamila feels the weight of her son, who is departing this life. Earlier, she told him to sleep. Now, she tries to keep him awake. She tells him a story, a story about a little boy who will grow up. It's a lie, like all stories.

Their water supply ran out a long time ago.

The child's lips are rough as the wood of the boat. Jamila stares at the dark, forsaken gap between them. She bends and lets some of her own saliva pass through her son's lips. The sea is like a mine now, closed over their heads, the house of the devil. The depths have come up to the surface. She has felt desperation, terror. Now she is simply waiting for destiny. The last face of history. Her flesh furrowed by salt spray, she looks for her destiny in a place where there's no longer a horizon, just sea. What was once the sea of salvation has become a circle of wet fire. A black heart.

She set aside the money for this trip, Omar's dinars, Nonno Mussa's euros and dollars, crumpled, sweaty paper. Like the other passengers, she handed it all over for this boat with no one at its helm. Nothing but a plastic eye and tanks of diesel fuel, almost all of them empty at this point. No one knows the sea. Only a few of them will stay afloat. They are creatures of sand.

The young Somali man is hallucinating. He has a skin disease, bloody pustules he can't stop scratching. He's got a high fever and thrashes about as if possessed by an evil spirit. He's stripped off his clothes. It's terrible to see a naked boy trying to scramble over other bodies. The others are tired of him. They want to throw him in the water. They scream that Somalis are all pirates.

The Somali spits in the water, yells that the sea is to blame for his illness, the white mud that floats on the waters of Mogadishu, the barrels of waste left on the sea floor by ships from the rich world. Now he waves his arms about as if he were holding a machete. That was his work, cutting down trees, burying them and burning them in the sand to make charcoal. He laughs, says everything will die, that animals no longer have trees and pasture. The charcoal is to blame. No one thinks of the future. Everyone thinks about survival nowadays and it doesn't matter if you kill your country. The poor can't afford to think about the future. He laughs, says they are in such a hurry to sell charcoal from their trees that they shovel it into bags before it's done burning and sometimes the ships catch fire. He howls, scratches himself, rolls like burning charcoal. He lifts the flare launcher into the air and shoots off the last flare. This time it climbs into the sky, incredibly high, a perfect trajectory, an arc of luminous drops.

Everyone looks at the firework display. Everyone expresses thanks for the divine manifestation. Everyone wakes from the antechamber of death. They cheer for the incendiary Somali. Someone will see them. A ship full of sailors dressed in white uniforms will come to save them, will lift them with gloved hands, give them platefuls of delicacies and miraculous ointments for the blisters on their mouths.

Like squid around a fishing light, they sit there watching the sea in the dark.

★　　★　　★

Farid grows lighter and lighter until he's a child made of bamboo, of hollow wood. His legs are two swaying reeds ending in two dirty feet. Ages ago, Jamila took off his sandals. *Move your toes*, she told him. It was one of the last things the child did – tried to move those little feet, keep those toes alive. Now his breath smells like coal, a hoarse rattle that comes up from the depths, that seems to come from a much bigger, older body. Maybe the child has aged during the journey.

Jamila caresses his forehead and his salt-stiff hair, pulls him to her. Farid's eyes are half closed. Jamila looks at those moving white fissures. They seek her. He's calm now, like when he's about to fall asleep, the day's last struggle as his eyelids fall.

He's always been a calm child, a little man.

Jamila remembers when he would ask her permission to pee in the garden because he'd waited too long to make it to the bathroom. He'd open his legs and grab his little willy and she'd tell him to move a bit further from the house, but he was afraid of the dark, afraid to leave the circle of light made by the light bulb.

Now and then, Omar pissed in the garden, too. Jamila scolded him. The stink would come into the house with the heat. Omar laughed, his white teeth shining through the dark. Father and son stood spraying side by side, large and small united in that manly gesture. Sometimes they would cross their sprays. Other times they'd compare the two wet holes in the sand.

Jamila doesn't know why she's thinking of something so stupid.

She has so many more important memories. Instead, she thinks of those two jets of piss in her garden, and the way she'd yell, *Go further away! Further away! My flowers will stink and dry up!*

Jamila is a dying insect. Her heart is a lantern that refuses to go out. How much longer must it endure? To illuminate Farid's night.

One day, she hung a little leather sack round his neck, velvety soft. She chased away the ghosts, blew in all the best dreams.

When she saw the sea, it looked big and wet, but nothing more. An easy land with no weapons. A blessing. She didn't know it was endless, that it would holler from all sides. For days and nights its mute black face rising and falling with the waves. Her hands are puckered like uncovered roots. She clutches her son, her dried desert fruit.

At home, Farid played with pieces of aerial, wire scraps his father no longer needed.

In Italy, Jamila will send him to school. She has friends in the north. She'll try to reach them. They came by sea, too, but with a smaller, faster boat. They're doing well now. They have a laundry in a neighbourhood full of Chinese hairdressers. At the beginning, it was terrible. They slept in the park and were always on the run. She and Farid will receive better treatment. They aren't illegals. They're refugees, fleeing a war. They will have a temporary residence permit. They'll request asylum. She'll find a job and learn Italian at night school. One day, maybe, she'll go back home. She'll sit down and look at her life. Farid will have grown by then, with his father's prominent rear and narrow shoulders. The same sheepish smile. He'll be good with electricity, like Omar. He has the same long fingers like screwdrivers.

The gazelle is on the sea. There's no knowing how, but she's there, stock still on the blue blade of the waves, resting regally as if on a dune. She turns to look at Farid, her shining ringed horns motionless.

They are small, brave, dignified animals, with slender legs, tight muscles and a black stripe along their backs that trembles when danger is near. They're the desert's most magnificent ornament. Their acute hearing cuts through the silence. Their eyes are magic, with transparent corneas and celebrated shining pupils that see eagles in the sky and African painted dogs hiding in the bushes. During the dry season, when all the other animals leave the desert regions and the burnt steppes, they remain loyal to their place, and often their meat nourishes big carnivores that would otherwise die. They have a slightly odd way of running, as if they aren't touching the sand. They leave a trail of little round foot-prints like coins. They're very fast. They must be, to survive. Now and then, they stop and look back, like children do, and this curiosity can be fatal. Mauled at the neck, a gazelle never struggles, but simply allows itself to be dragged away and killed. Arab poets have eulogized them, and praised their innocent gaze as the hallmark of beauty.

As he dies, Farid thinks of the gazelle, her eyes that come so close to his own, her mouth with its flat teeth eating from his hand in the pistachio grove.

As Farid dies, Jamila continues holding him, continues to sing. She doesn't want the others to notice. They're wicked now. She saw the bodies they threw into the sea. She's gone past life and is still here. She knows that it's better this way, better that her heart held out. Her final fear had been that she would die before her child, allow him to fall from her arms. Allow him to feel the immense solitude of the sea. The black heart.

Once, in the desert, she saw a fennec cub beside its dead mother, alone, surrounded by the calls of nocturnal predators as they calmly crept near.

Her son's neck is stretched out like a slaughtered animal's. She looks at the amulet, which no longer moves.

None of the passengers on this boat will ever set foot on land. They're down to the last drop of diesel. They've lost their course. A ship will pass in the distance but will not stop.

Hands grasp for the surface. Lungs burst without a sound. Bodies tumble towards the depths, sway like monkeys on lost vines. Sand creatures swollen with sea and shredded by the hunger of the depths.

The seaside restaurant is empty.

There's no one but a police official absorbed in a

newspaper as he consumes his single plate of cheese pasta beneath the trellis.

The owner of the restaurant has stepped out onto the beach, a white apron over his name-bearing T-shirt. Hands on his hips, he looks at the sea.

Vito walks along the beach.

A dead jellyfish lies next to a plastic bag covered with tar.

This year, the sea is a wall of jellyfish.

That's not why the tourists won't come.

Vito walks along the beach.

He saw those overladen boats that stank like jars of mackerel. Guys from North Africa, veterans of the wars there, veterans of refugee camps, stowaways. He saw their dazed eyes, the hand-over-hand passage of children who'd survived the voyage, hypothermia sufferers with silver blankets. He saw fear of the sea and fear of land.

He saw the strength of those wretches: *I want to work. I want to work. I want to work in France, in northern Europe.*

He saw their determination and their purity. The beauty in their eyes, the white of their teeth.

He saw the degradation, the animal-like conditions.

Young men standing with their backs against a wall while soldiers took away their shoelaces and belts.

He saw the race to help them, used clothes for the children, donations from poor people pissed-off because Jesus Christ always turns to them.

He saw the overflowing camps, the fear of disease, the protesters who blocked the piers and landing places, and then started it all over again by throwing themselves into the sea at night to pull out those wretches who didn't know how to swim.

There's no way of knowing who you'll end up saving. It might be some jailbird who'll steal your mobile phone, drink-drive in the wrong lane, rape some nurse heading home after the night shift.

Vito has heard this kind of talk, jumbled, crude. The anger of poor people against other poor people.

Saving your killer – perhaps that is charity. But here, no one is a saint. And the world shouldn't need martyrs, just more equity.

Angelina is at the window. She is waiting for her son, who's not on his way back. It doesn't matter. She knows that one day he will not come back. That's life.

She may not have been a good mother. She was like a lizard whose tail had been cut off. Vito was her new tail.

But how can one hope?

The TV is off. It's an old TV; it doesn't work well; it suffers when there's wind or rain. They should get a new TV, a new aerial. But anyway, this is just their summer house.

Angelina is waiting for the war to end, for the actor of a thousand faces to be captured and tried.

She saw the NATO bombings, heard the usual *There will be no civilian targets*. They didn't even spare the factory that supplied oxygen tanks to the hospital.

She saw the tricks, Green Square full of rebels, a fake created by the television. A film set.

She saw the warriors with their bandanas, children carrying machine guns. She stretched her hand out towards the television as if to stop them.

Their city destroyed, the bullet-ridden walls, the holes left behind by explosions. Palm trees white with debris.

Her mother, Santa, said, *They're shooting at us.*

We are Tripolini. We aren't from here, and we aren't from there. We're stuck in the sea like those people with nowhere to land.

They saw the rebels, regular people. Girls who did

not wear the veil speaking on the radio, university students with machine guns and beach sandals.

They saw the old Senussi flag.

They saw child soldiers. The little loyalists, drafted for a few dinars, were killed on their knees, a bullet to the base of their skull like animals in the savannah.

They saw a woman news reader with a veil, bearing a gun.

They saw bare-handed mine removers dressed in shorts and sweating like farmers in their fields.

What will happen to all of those weapons afterwards?

She woke up with that thought in the night.

They will move on to another war. Nerve gas and mustard gas. The colonel's arsenal, wooden cases of machine guns, mines, rockets, all with the same surreal label: *Ministry of Agriculture*.

Fields sown with mines. This is the harvest.

Every night a new boat, human fertilizer, escapees from hunger, from war.

It's a late summer day of blooming caper plants and enchantment. A truce after three stormy days. The beach is a rubbish dump for pieces of wood, the remains of boats that never arrived. A war museum on the crushed stone beach. Vito picks through it, combing for bits to save.

He goes back and forth along the beach, drags crooked boards and scraps of rugs.

He stops to pick up a little leather pouch that looks like a jewellery bag. He has a hard time opening it because of the knots in the tightly wound cord. He sticks in a finger. Nothing except something that feels like wet wool and a few beads. He throws it into his bag with the rest.

On the island, there is a cemetery for the unknown dead. Some good man rubbed wild mint under his nose so as not to be overcome by the smell and gathered the bodies the sea had delivered. He planted crosses. Someone else removed them, but it doesn't matter. The poor have only one God. Every day he drowns with them and then causes wild garlic and beach poppies to grow up amongst the mounds. Vito has walked there. It's a bare place, wind-beaten and without sorrow. The sea scours everything. No mothers come here to cry. No one brings flowers. Just little thoughts from strangers, tourists who leave a note, a toy. Vito sits down, imagines the bones below the field like the skeleton of a ship turned upside down.

He thinks about the turtles that come up onto the

beach to lay their eggs. The island is a refuge for marine life. In a while, the eggs will hatch. Vito has seen it before, the little turtles going after the tide, running towards the sea to save themselves from death.

At home later on, he nails his gatherings to a board. The page of a diary in Arabic. A shirtsleeve. A doll's arm.

It's a job with no tangible meaning, dictated by the uncredited desperation that afflicts him.

This is how he will spend the last days of their summer here on the island. In the shed.

He has to decide what to do with his life, whether to waste it or to make it somehow bear fruit.

His mother said, *You have to find a place inside you and around you, a place that is right for you, at least in part.*

Vito can't stand it when she does that. When she looks at the sea and doesn't talk, her fists deep in the pockets of her cardigan.

He is simply unable to make a decision. He's thought about it but hasn't made up his mind. Maybe he will remain a dunce. Maybe he's not that smart. In any case, he's slow. He needs time.

Vito drags things, glues things. Pieces of those aborted escapes.

He doesn't know why he's doing this. He's looking

for a place. He'd like to capture something. Lives that never reached their destination.

He thinks of his mother's eyes resting on the sea, following the lost course of the ball of wool wound round her throat. Since their trip to Tripoli she's looked only for joy. She took up cooking – fig pies, pasta casseroles. She arranged sprigs of broom in vases. She wants there to be things for him to remember. The feeling of a house to come back to with his eyes closed, just to take a breath.

Angelina comes in, asks why he didn't come for lunch. She looks at the immense panel of sea remains, bits of wood nailed on, scraps of denim stuck on with glue.

She looks at the motionless explosion.

'Have you taken up art?'

Vito shrugs. His hands are black. There's glue in his hair. He leans against the wall near the case of old bottles, rubs his eyes with his wrists, kicks the dust.

He won't let his mother near. He keeps her at a distance, in the shadows. He speaks to himself.

'I stopped a shipwreck.'

Vito has gathered memory. Of a blue gas tank, a shoe. *Someone will need this someday. Someday, a black Italian man will want to look back at the sea of his ancestors and find something. A trace of their passage. Like a suspension bridge.*

Angelina cannot look at her son. It is beyond her. It would be like looking at him when he's making love.

She goes to the big blue panel.

She touches those poor encrusted things, marine relics washed by salt. A shipwreck sculpted in their tool shed. It's striking. It's like an intact archaeological site. A world saved.

Angelina looks at the sea her son has recreated, the things he chose from the beach, from history. An interior space in the undertow of the world.

She looks at the leather pouch nailed in the centre.

She knows it's a charm, the kind mothers in the Sahara prepare at night beneath the watchful eyes of the stars and put round their children's necks to ward away the evil eyes of death.

She rubs her nose against it like an animal. She hears the sound of the sea, so similar to the sound of blood.

Then it happened.

What month was it? October, always October. The month of their banishment. The month of her birthday. Angelina had thought she might not make it to that birthday alive. One of those thoughts that worms its way in and nibbles away at you. She had made a sort of will, put her affairs in order, bank statements and settled bills out in plain sight.

Vito was gone. That may have been what did it. The feeling of death. *I've raised him. Now I can go.* There was nothing to be done about the mistakes she'd made, so many of them, and yet not so many at all when you lined them up at night, while you emptied a drawer and tidied up the disaster. The photos from Africa and the rest – old bus tickets, an envelope with medical exams, the writing of a certain man who had believed he loved you for a certain time.

She also wrote a long letter to Vito. *My love*, it began. *My son*, it began. One of those nighttime letters that don't go anywhere, that dig deep as the street sweepers pass by beneath the house. That go too far. Where it's not right to go.

A mother has to stay one step behind.

That night, she smoked a poisonous number of cigarettes. In the morning, she threw away the packet along with the letter. A vehement gesture.

She cleaned the refrigerator. She got rid of every unworthy thing. Old notes, a packet of condoms that had not been used by their expiry date and that she had held on to as a symbol of sexual love, of possibilities. Ridiculous. Like so many ridiculous things. Her thoughts, above all. Like a broom scratching over the patio.

She planted perennials in the flowerpots. The house was clean. For him, if he came back. She lay down on the bed, her feet bare. To see what her cadaver would be like. And she waited a long time.

She thought only of Vito, of Vito beside her.

She went to the window.

It was her birthday. She was alive. Naturally, it had been nothing but anxiety.

Vito called from London. She could hear the ruckus of the Italian café where he worked.

'Happy birthday, Mum.'

Half an hour later, he called again.

'Did you hear the news, Mum? They killed him.'

Angelina felt the blows. An entire machine gun's worth.

'Who? Who did they kill?'

She thought of Vito in London, of the attacks, the Underground, the crowded square in front of the Tate Gallery where he spent his Sundays.

'Gaddafi. They killed Gaddafi.'

'Oh.'

She fell onto a carpet of flower petals, light, immortal.

That was the October crime.

She didn't go online to see the mob and the bloody rat's flight into a hole in the cement. She knows how dictators end their days. Flesh dragged along like an eraser. Senseless posthumous rage. No joy, just a macabre trophy that soils the living.

Memory is chalk on bloody pavements.

We're free. Hurrah, hurrah.